I0684542

Blood
of
Quetzalcoatl

A Mario Martinez Mystery

Book One of the Aztec Series

By Annette Shelley

Blood of Quetzalcoatl
Copyright © 2010 by Annette Shelley
Printed in the United States of America
By Legends Press.

ISBN 13: 978-0-9841325-1-5
ISBN 10: 0-9841325-1-1

www.annetteshelley.com

Dedication
To Dad

Acknowledgements
To my friends and supporters: Mom, Dad and Mark
Pat Moon, Paula Wagner, Kym Roberts, Cindy Kennedy,
Jenny Murphy, Karen Wood, Jim Merideth and Geri Srikanth
Special thanks to the late Joe Crosson who was with me
when I first "met" Mario Martinez nearly ten years ago and
encouraged me to pursue and finish this.

Spanish Phrases Glossary

Dear Readers,

I used a few simple Spanish phrases in the book and include this brief glossary here for your reference. Enjoy!   Annette

Amigo - friend
Andale - hurry
Aqui – here
Attencion – attention
Aztecas - Aztecs
Bella –   beautiful
Bueno - good
Buenos Dias - good day
Buenos noches – good evening/night
Calle - street
Churros – cookies with cinnamon and sugar on top
Cinco - five
Cincuenta - fifty
Comprende – understand
Cuanto – how much?
Dias – day
El – masculine form of the
Es - is
Flan – Mexican pastry
Gente – People
Hasta manana – until tomorrow
Hola – hello
Huitzilopochtli – Aztec god of war and sacrifice
La – feminine form of the
Magnifico - magnificent
Manana – tomorrow
Mayor – main, primary, major
Menudo – stew made from tripe
Mi – my

Muertos - the dead
Museo - museum
Nada – nothing
Noche - night
Noche Triste – Night of Sorrows
Nombre - name
Numero - number
Palacia – palace
Partido – Political party
Peso – Mexican penny
Policia - police
Por favor – if you please, please
Presidente – President
Problemo – problem
Pulque – hallucinogenic mixture made from cactus pulp
Que - what
Quiere - want
Quetzalcoatl – Aztec Feathered Serpent god
Rapido – quick, fast
Salas – floors or levels in a building
Senor – sir
Senora – ma'am, married woman
Senorita – young woman, unmarried
Si- yes
Stupido - stupid
Tamales – beef rolled in a tortilla and fried
Te - you
Templo - temple
Touristas - tourists
Tres – three
Triste - sad
Uno - one
Y – and
Yo no se – I don't know
Zocalo – city center of Mexico City

DAY ONE

One

M ario Martinez stood in the crammed subway car with his back pressed against the center pole. He glanced over the top of his newspaper at the wrinkled woman hunched in the handicapped seat. Her long stained skirt covered thick legs, knotted hands rested in her lap.

Several boys with identical black shirts and cutoff jeans pressed themselves against the wall. The tallest of the three had a menacing barbed wire mark encircling his neck and each had symbols tattooed on their skulls bleeding through buzz haircuts. Mario hated despised the gangs taking over Mexico City. Glancing at his watch, he tossed his paper aside and caught a faint whiff of cheap perfume and aftershave, sweat and greasy food as he pushed his way toward the doors. Once the train stopped, he turned to the old woman, took her hand and helped her up. "After you."

She fumbled around with several crumpled sacks gathered at her feet. "*Gracias*."

Impatient people behind him mumbled complaints about the delay. He didn't care. Once the old lady safely reached the platform, Mario leapt into the crowded Metro station and ran to the staircase next to the overcrowded escalator.

Ascending the subterranean tunnel, he exited on the surface street above, where a hot blast of stale July air reeking of fast food and pollution hit him in the face.

On the streets of Mexico City, Mario passed enormous stone monuments and skyscrapers, dodged in and out of hundreds of thick white tents busy street vendors pitched earlier that morning. At the outer walls of the city center, or *Zocalo*, he picked up speed and rounded the corner near Cathedral Metropolitano with only a minute to spare before he would officially be late to work.

Dozens of summer patrons waited in a long line to get a glimpse of *El Templo Mayor*, one of the largest remaining Aztec ruins in the world. Out of breath, Mario pushed his way past the crowd. "Pardon, excuse me, thank you." He spoke English for the benefit of visitors from the United States and Europe.

The tourists moved aside and Mario approached the gate. He straightened his tie, cinching it tight around his neck, slicked his wavy black hair back with his palms, wiped his face off and smiled at the girl in the ticket booth. "*Buenos dias.*"

Lupe stuffed her pudgy mouth full of Mexican cookies called *churros.* She licked powdered sugar from her lips and mumbled. "Mmm *dias.*" She buzzed him in.

Mario pinned the gold star on his lapel. It resembled a local police badge just enough to keep most guests under control. He secured his gun in the holster and headed toward the precarious walking bridge that always made him feel a little sick. Even today, the slight breeze caused the wooden planks to wobble. He held his breath and stepped out, gripped the thick rope handrails on either side and tried not to look down any longer than his job required. Three long steps later, he stood safe on the other side.

Templo Mayor was an exciting place to work, unless you had a fear of heights. Mario hated his phobia, but overcame it daily. His morning job involved looking around to make sure nothing got disturbed overnight.

His view was always obstructed by scaffolding from the never-ending construction projects around the site. While the world's most talented archeologists and scholars unearthed chipped pottery shards, ancient bone fragments and other treasures from antiquity, construction workers frantically rebuilt what they destroyed. The media never strayed far from the site either, anxious to report new historical discoveries in the former Aztec capitol as soon as they occurred.

A quick glance of the lower rooms with a sweep with his flashlight told him instantly whether or not he needed to clear the area of any vagrants or other unwanted visitors. Ever since the city put up the barbed wire fence around the property, homeless hadn't been a problem. At least that's what his boss told him. Mario wouldn't know firsthand. He only started the job two weeks ago.

The wind picked up, swaying the bridge beneath him. Mario wiped the sweat off his forehead and clutched the ropes tighter. His stomach churned. He stopped on a corner wooden platform until he could get his equilibrium under control. From this vantage point, he could see into several of the lower rooms without moving a muscle.

After shining his light and finding nothing out of the ordinary, Mario regained his bearings and hurried around the far side of the property. He checked his watch. Only five more minutes until the gates opened and tourists would stomp all over him to get into the ruins, especially the famed Eagle Chamber.

Considered the prize of *Templo Mayor*, the room dedicated to Eagle once served as the site for the bloody human sacrifices for which the Aztecs had become infamous. In ancient times, spiritual leaders used the Eagle Chamber for ritual prayer and considered this the most sacred area of the entire temple complex. Archaeologists substantiated sacrificial evidence through extensive carbon testing on the soil which showed remnants of blood, animal remains, and various sacred foods. Now the site held nothing but barren stone and dirt floors, crumbling walls and stairs typical of traditional Aztec architecture.

Mario always felt relieved by the time he reached eagle Chamber because the walkway here was steadier than any of the others. His stomach calmed down. He shined his flashlight into each corner under several stone structures. His job was routine and mundane, day in and day out.

Today was different. He scanned the far right wall and moved his light toward the center of the earthen room, something strange caught his eye - a grisly Aztec reenactment of blood and sacrifice.

The staff probably created the display for the amusement of today's tourists. *Strange the boss never mentioned it.* Mario's hand rested on his gun, but he never thought to draw. He started walking away, but stopped and decided to take a closer look, turned the flashlight on high.

A lifeless torso split from neck to navel lay at the bottom of the stone steps. Mario's eyes traced the crimson trail to the top of the altar where a severed head with long black hair dangled atop an earthen pillar. A primitively

8

carved stone cup filled with some internal organ spilled over in a bloody mess. He stepped closer, squinted his eyes, gripped the handrail with his left hand, running the tips of his right fingers over his gun handle. He studied the scene for a few moments before the full impact registered in his brain. His eyes settled on the blood streaked body clothed in a white modern sundress. A large handbag and one flimsy violet colored ladies sandal with a big yellow sunflower in the middle tossed off to one side suggested a more contemporary crime.

The images vaguely registered in his still sleepy brain, and cold chills rushed through his torso. He knew that shoe. He recognized the dress too, and the purse. They didn't belong to any Aztecs, either. A guttural cry rose up from his center. "No!"

Two

Benito Juarez recently became the youngest Presidente in Mexican history. Born of migrant farm workers, his father bestowed his son with the perfect name to help him rise beyond his allotted station in life. Today, in his first official cabinet meeting since the election, Bene Juarez stood at the head of a long mahogany table in the private presidential conference room on the top floor of the Palacio, regally flanked on either side by Mexican flags. He never dreamed this day would come to pass and Bene felt grateful for his staunch supporters and benefactors. "Thank you everyone for all your hard work during my campaign. I look forward to working with each of you and—"

Before finishing his sentiment, the mahogany doors burst open and a heavily armed palace guard loomed over the proceeding. "*Senor Presidente*."

A stern scowl crossed Benito's normally handsome face. "What are you doing? I told you not to disturbed us under any circumstance."

The guard lowered his eyes. "Pardon, *Senor*, but I'm afraid there is an emergency."

The men erupted in gasps and whispers.

Bene lifted his hand to quiet them. "Gentlemen please, I'm sure it's nothing."

The room fell silent.

Taking a seat in the high backed chair at the head of the table, Benito knit his fingers together, tightened his jaw. "What kind of emergency? This better be good."

The guard wrung his hands. "*Senor Presidente*, I'm afraid this is serious…very serious."

During his limited time in office, Bene had enough experience to know the younger guards often overreacted. He laughed. "I'm sure. So tell us. What happened?"

The guard sighed. "*Senor*, I believe I should speak to you alone."

Bene drew a deep breath, pushed himself back from the table and stood. "Gentlemen, I'm afraid duty calls. I'm sure this won't take long though, so if you'd like to take a break, we can resume again in a few—"

The guard interrupted again. "No disrespect, *Senor Presidente*, but you cannot return to this meeting today."

Bene knew he should be furious at such blatant disregard for his position, but something about the look on the guard's face told him he needed to pay attention. A sick feeling settled in the pit of his stomach. The position of *Presidente* would likely hold many stressful days. He didn't realize today would be among them. "Fine. Gentlemen, take a break, stay if you want, or we can finish up tomorrow."

Several men stood up, others pulled out cell phones and laptops and a few left the room.

Bene followed the guard out into the hallway. "This better be good, or you'll be looking for a new post."

"Understood, *Senor Presidente*. Right this way, *por favor*." The guard led Bene down the wood paneled hallway to a small office where his long time confidant and advisor Rita sat at her desk.

The second she saw Benito standing in the door, Rita hung up her phone. Black streaks ran down her face, her eyes appeared swollen from tears. "*Senor Presidente…*"

"Rita?" Since childhood, Bene could only recall one other time when she looked this upset - the day his mother died. Cold stillness rushed through his torso. "What's wrong?"

She pulled a tissue from a box, wiped her eyes.

Benito turned to the guard. "Leave us."

The guard bowed and closed the door behind him. "*Si, Senor.*"

Rita's curtains were drawn tight, the normal cheery mood in her office seemed drab and depressing. "What's going on?"

Rita sniffed. "I don't know how to tell you this."

His mind raced. "Is it my father? He didn't have a heart attack, did he?"

Rita shook her head. "No, *Senor*."

"Well what then?" He reached across her desk, grabbed her forearms. "Are you okay?"

Rita blew her nose again and kept crying. "Something's happened, Bene."

His chest tightened, his mouth felt dry. "What?"

"At *Templo Mayor*…today…" Her words were broken, inarticulate. "…a…murder."

Murder? Did he hear her right? No. Couldn't be. "Murder?"

"Uh huh."

Such a scandal would topple the tourism industry if the national media got wind of it. "Before hours? Were there witnesses? Do I need to call the press and make a statement?"

"Stop, Bene. Listen to me." Her tears wrinkled the papers on her desk. "Nobody saw the body."

Good, this he could handle. "Fine, then we'll close the gates, reopen at noon, give everyone a peso or two off admission—"

Rita clutched his hands. "It was…Angela."

Angela? The name didn't hit him at first. He wrinkled his brow. He couldn't equate the name Angela with the word *murder*. This must be a mistake. "Angela?" His mind slowly filled in the pieces to the puzzle. "No."

Rita sniffed. "*Si.*"

His hands shook. He couldn't stop them. "Angela? Mi Angela? *Mi Angel?*" Tears filled his eyes, rage overshadowed his heart. He fell into the chair across from Rita's desk. "No. This cannot be."

"*Sí*." Rita walked around her desk, put her arms around the man she'd known since childhood. "Angela is dead."

Bene doubled over, wishing he could squeeze the news of Angela's death from his body and mind. He broke down in wrenching sobs, fell forward in the chair and pounded his fists on the desk. "Why Rita? How could this happen? *Por favor*, tell me this isn't true."

Rita braced herself on his shoulders. "Oh Benito, there are so many evil people in the world."

He held his head in his hands, his pulse quickened to dizzying levels. "What happened? How?"

"I'm not sure. The *policia* are investigating. They said it looked like she'd been sacrificed to the gods of old in an authentic Aztec ritual."

Repulsive images filled Bene's mind. He couldn't imagine Angela associated with such cruelty. His entire body shook while he contemplated how his angel spent her last moments on Earth. Bitter tears wrenched from his eyes. "This is a mistake."

Rita patted his shoulder. "I am so sorry."

Someone knocked on the office door and swung it open. Benito's father, Juarez Senior, stood in the foyer. "What the hell is going on around here? Why aren't you in the meeting? Where did everyone run off to?"

Bene leapt out of the chair and shoved his father against the open door, pressing his index finger into his old man's chest. "You did this," he screamed. "You killed her you son-of-a-bitch."

Juarez Senior appeared shocked until he got his bearings, grabbed Bene's lapels. "Get your hands off me. Have you gone mad?"

Bene stood within an inch of his father's face. "Angela, Papa. She is dead. Murdered. You wanted this all along, didn't you?"

Office doors up and down the hallway swung open and a crowd gathered, staring at the spectacle.

The elder Juarez cleared his throat, brushed off his suit jacket and grabbed Bene by the shoulders. "What do you mean, son? Calm down."

Benito brushed his father's hands away. "Get away from me."

Backed against the wall, Rita carefully stepped forward, cleared her throat. "Angela Martinez was found dead this morning at the *Templo Mayor*, *Senor* Juarez."

Bene lunged at his father again, shoving him in the shoulder. "Whether or not you killed her yourself doesn't matter. You never wanted her. You wished this on her."

"No," Juarez Senior said.

Bene pointed into the hall. "Get out of here. Get out of my sight. I hate you and I never want to see you again."

Juarez Senior put his hands up in surrender, backed away and turned to the gathered crowd. "What are you looking at? This is between me and my son."

The staff cowered back into their offices and Rita closed her door. "You know your father had nothing to do with this. Please, try and calm down—"

Bene fell back into the chair. "He hated her. He didn't want me to be seen with her, he called her a radical."

Rita wiped fresh tears from her eyes. "I'm sure he didn't mean it."

"He did." Bene took a few deep breaths. He finally had reason to voice his long repressed opinion. "What am I going to do?"

She hugged him again. "Eventually you will heal. I promise."

"No I won't. There is...*was*... nobody like my Angel." *Dear God!* Referring to the love of his life in past tense was unbearable. Bene feared what he would do to those responsible. His vengeance would ensure he could never continue on as *Presidente*, but he didn't care. Someone would pay dearly for ruining his life and dashing his hopes for the future. "Who found her?"

"The guard."

The guard. A new wave of panic settled over him. "Oh no. You don't mean the *new* guard, do you?"

Rita shrugged. "I don't know. They told me the guard found her while making rounds this morning."

Bene's hands trembled. His troubles compounding by the second. "Call *Templo Mayor*. Bring that guard to me at once. Tell them this is an emergency."

Three

The little boy stared up at the tall fat man who held out more money than he'd ever seen in his short life– enough to feed his entire family for quite some time. He glanced over his shoulder toward the busy street vendors and saw his mother picking out tortillas for dinner tonight. She wouldn't like him wandering off like this until he brought the money. The man held up two burlap sacks. He spoke in a mean voice. "*Comprende*?"

He nodded and held out his hands for the pesos. He needed to hurry before his mom caught him. "*Si*."

The stranger scowled. "You sure you know what to do?" "*Si*."

"And you know not to tell anyone about this, right?"

He shook his outstretched hands. "*Si*."

"*Aqui*." He handed over the pesos.

The little boy stuffed the money deep in his pockets and lifted the cloth sacks, on in each hand. They felt heavier than what he expected, but not too heavy, considering the pay. Something dripped out of one of them. Red paint splashed the clean shirt his mom put on him this morning. His mother might yell at him for ruining his clothes, but once she saw the money, everything would be alright.

The man never answered his question. Instead, he clapped his hands and brushed the boy away like a stray dog. "*Andale*, hurry, run."

The little boy ran through the *Zocalo* into the big church in the middle of the square. Around the far right side, a set of steep stone stairs led down a narrow passageway to someplace underground. A red and white sign marked the spot exactly as the man told him. By now his arms ached from the weight of the load. He dragged the bags down the stairs, the contents pounded against the stone steps. Too exhausted to lift them any higher, he hoped he didn't break anything. More liquid leaked out of the bottom of the sack. Whatever was in there must be ruined already. He hoped he wouldn't get in trouble.

At the bottom of the stairs, he knocked on the door. It creaked open. He peeked inside. "*Hola*?"

Big meaty hands reached through the dark, ripped the bags from his tiny hands, covered his mouth and restrained his arms. The sound of a heavy thud filled his ears. His world went black.

Four

Mario threw up twice, and dry heaved a third time before regaining his bearings. With no concern whatsoever about danger or heights, he ran back to the entrance of *Templo Mayor* just as Lupe opened the gates for the day. "Stop! Don't do that!"

"Do what?" She pushed the button allowing a middle aged couple to walk inside.

He stepped forward, pushing the pair back with his palms. "Excuse me, *Senor, Senora*, but we're not quite ready to open yet."

The couple seemed incensed. "But we've been waiting here for forty minutes," the woman complained.

"I understand, ma'am, but there's been a delay. If you'll please step outside…" He corralled them out and slammed the door, locked the gate. Several people waved their tickets and mumbled.

Lupe pried her hefty body from her seat and squeezed through the door of her guard shack. "What do you think you're doing? Are you nuts? The Director is gonna—"

Turning his back to the disgruntled crowd, Mario rubbed his face with trembling hands, his eyes filled with tears. "Don't let anyone in here. Call the police."
        ***

Within minutes, several heavily armed uniformed policia officers arrived and barricaded the gates. The waiting crowd received refunds and rain checks and were asked to return later. Since Mario made the discovery, the police asked him to show them the scene. He didn't think he could. Life as he knew it was over. Nothing would be the same ever again.

He led them toward the far side of the property, knowing this single incident might affect him for the rest of his days. He demanded justice, with or without police. For now, he planned to assist law enforcement, but if necessary, he would take matters into his own hands.

One of the officers shined a light into the Eagle Chamber. "Where?"

Mario's jaw dropped open. To his shock, only a single trail of blood remained, but the body and all other evidence disappeared. Panic ripped through his torso. Did he imagine all this? He wished. "I don't know. I swear the body was here just a few minutes ago."

Down below, only the ladies sandal, a torn piece of the white cloth dress and the handbag remained *What happened to the body?* He wasn't gone more than five minutes, ten tops. Nobody could possibly remove a corpse so quickly in such a crowded public venue. No way.

The officer raised his eyebrows and sketched notes in his pad. "Uh huh, and what exactly did you see?"

Mario didn't appreciate the patronizing tone, but he would do the same if he were in the officer's shoes. He felt like a complete fool. "I saw a woman down there a few minutes ago. Right there. *I saw her.* I swear."

"Okay…" The officer rolled his eyes and chuckled.

He couldn't believe this. His legs went numb. He pressed his palm to his forehead and grabbed a handrail to stop his dizzy head from pounding any harder. "I saw blood dripping, the body torn to shreds, and right there, I saw…"

"*Si?*" The officer jotted notes in his pad.

Mario glanced at the altar where the head and the internal organs were carefully displayed only minutes earlier. *They disappeared into thin air.* "Hey. The head…I saw it there." He pointed to the bloody spot.

The officer lowered his pad and leaned into the rail to take a closer look. "Where?"

"There." He noticed another line of blood trailing off the side of the stone steps in the other direction. "And that bowl held some kind of internal organs."

"You mean the *empty* one?" the officer teased.

Red liquid dripped over the edges of the ancient clay pot. "You can see the blood though." Mario defended himself.

"*If* that's real blood down there," the officer noted. "Could be a demonstration the museum's doing, right?"

Mario gritted his teeth and tried not to lose it. He didn't want to explain how he thought the same thing when he first saw it. That would only make matters worse. "It's real," he snapped. "I'm telling you."

19

The officer made a note. "Had you seen the victim in here before?"

How many times do I have to repeat myself? "The ruins were closed for the night, *senor*. I found the body right before Lupe opened the gates this morning." While giving his interview, he watched two officers climb down inside the exhibit and take photographs and blood samples. They collected the sandals and purse and bagged everything up.

The officer jotted more notes. "So you're saying you did not see the victim in here prior to finding the body?"

Mario lowered his eyes. "No."

"You never saw this person walking around the property? Visiting the ruins before?"

He shook his head. "No, never. Not since I've worked here, anyway."

The officer made more notes. "And you do not know the victim's identity, correct?"

Mario's stomach clenched tight. He lurched forward, dry heaving again.

The officer stepped closer, put a hand on his shoulder. "You okay?"

He wiped his mouth on his sleeve. "*Si, senor.*"

The officer picked up his pad again. "You say you didn't know her, *si*?"

Mario wished his answer could be different. "I did."

The officer stopped writing. "You *did* know her?"

He nodded. "*Si.*"

"How?"

He gulped. "She was my sister."

***

After nearly collapsing from stress, the police escorted Mario inside the museum where he sat down and repeated his story to more *policia* telling them all he knew about Angela Martinez. He couldn't shed tears now, not because he felt ashamed. He couldn't feel his own face. His arms went numb, a great stillness settled over him. He felt trapped inside a nightmare. Angela didn't deserve this. Nobody did. "I swear I saw a body. I'm not crazy."

A loud knock interrupted the questioning officer before he could reply. Three heavily armed *palacio* guards carried automatic weapons and stood at attention by the door. "Mario Martinez?"

Mario would normally find these men intimidating, but not today. "*Si?*"

The largest of the three stepped forward and scowled. "*Senor Presidente* Benito Juarez requests you be brought to him immediately."

The questioning officer seemed puzzled. "Pardon, but why does *Senor Presidente* want him?"

The guard seemed in no mood for frivolities. "Official Presidential business, *por favor.*"

Mario knew exactly why the *Presidente* wanted to see him. The two of them should have met long before now under other circumstances.

Like a condemned prisoner, Mario silently allowed the men lead him away, down the hall, out the back of *Templo Mayor*. They hurried through back alleyway past a dozen other buildings. Armed Presidential guards stood by every few feet between the *Templo Mayor* and *palacio*. The entrance signified by an ornately carved wooden door with bronze hardware matched all the other palatial access points. Mario heard about these secret entryways, but like most regular working class citizens, he never saw them before today.

Inside the Presidential wing of the *palacio*, lush red carpet covered hallways lit with a series of elaborate chandeliers. More armed guards stood inside. Dozens of murals by famed artist Diego Rivera, husband of the better known Frieda Kahlo, lined the corridors, walls and staircases.

At the top of another stony stairwell, two more armed guards stood watch at every landing, despite limited access to the area. Officers flanked Mario on either side, holding his forearms while he ascended the remaining few flights of stairs. On the top floor, they walked down to the far end of the building. Double doors opened into the well appointed office of *Presidente* Benito Juarez.

El Presidente sat behind his desk. He didn't smile or frown. Immense strain reflected in his eyes. A handsome man by anyone's standards, Benito's rugged good looks and chiseled features made him a likely candidate for magazine model or TV star. Deep black eyes showed kindness and compassion. A well groomed beard and moustache accentuated his full mouth and perfect teeth.

Benito stood and extended his hand. "Thank you for coming."

Surprised by his immense height, Mario stood speechless for a moment.

"Guards, leave us please." Benito placed a reassuring hand on Mario's shoulder. "I know we don't know each other, but…" Tears filled his eyes.

Mario glanced down at the bear skin rug on the floor so the *Presidente* wouldn't see the tears welling in his own eyes. He felt bad enough for not meeting Benito before now. He owed the man a debt of gratitude for recent events. After finishing his mandatory year in the Mexican Army, Mario served for a short time as a military police officer and received the opportunity of a lifetime as lead guard for *Templo Mayor*. He planned to formally thank Benito for the strings he pulled during a meeting with Angela. Now that would never happen, he felt beyond awkward.

"Please sit down, *mi amigo*." Bene showed him to a heavy round table with high backed maroon leather cushioned chairs with large brass buttons. He pulled the seat out.

Mario gratefully sat, put his head in his hands and wept.

Five

A hooded attendant dragged the lifeless body of the little boy across the cold stone floor, down the pitch black passage into the assembly hall where hundreds of similarly dressed figures stood chanting.

On the high altar, a masked man dressed in feathers called him forward. "You have the remaining items?"

The attendant tossed the boy's body at the base of the altar, lifted the burlap sacks and bowed. "*Si*."

The leader was pleased. All was going as planned. He gestured his hooded guard with a curved finger. "Bring them forward."

23

Kneeling by the leaders feet, the man lifted the sacks and bowed. "Your Greatness, I present the heart and the head."

The feathered man eagerly accepted the offering and reached inside to present it to the congregation. Holding the lifeless head of a woman with long straight black hair in one hand, her heart in the other, he lifted the spoils high for all to see. "We succeeded, my brothers. We are now one step closer to solidifying our place in the cosmos for the next thousand years. *Vive Huitzilopochtli.*"

"*Vive Huitzilopochtli.*" The mob cheered and everyone joined in a unanimous chant. They stomped their feet, rattling the ancient stones the ancestors placed hundreds of years before.

The feathered man put the offerings atop a higher altar next to the decapitated bloodless body of the young woman sprawled out naked across the stones with the chest cavity splayed open and all internal organs removed and laid each relevant body part on a specific spot based on tradition and ritual. He turned to face the crowd. "Soon *Quetzalcoatl* will fall from grace and we will rule the world."

The chanting grew ever louder with each declaration. "*Vive Huitzilopochtli.*"

Once all the blood drained from the little boy's body, officials poured it into several cups and sent one down each row of the gathering, much like offering plates at traditional Catholic worship services. All in attendance drank and passed the cup to the next person until they were empty.

The feathered man stood center stage holding a solid gold goblet incrusted with rudimentary carved turquoise, reminiscent of those used by their Aztec ancestors. He lifted his cup and drank. "Brothers and sisters, Venus returned sooner than planned and we have much work to do in the coming days to prepare. We will not meet in this place again until the day of the event. Once we seize *Quetzalcoatl*, we will take him to a location you should all be aware of by now. We will reconvene at dusk tonight to await the gods' commands. Our window of opportunity is brief. We must work diligently to enact our plans for freedom. It is vital each of you understand your role and responsibilities. Remember, you made a vow to this organization, and I require your presence, regardless of circumstances. Tell your friends, families, employers you are not to be disturbed during these coming days. Do what you must to ensure your presence here. Each of you is critical to our success. Once our work is complete, in three days time, we will be free for the next fifty seven years to experience peace and joy on Earth and for the next thousand years our empire will be secured." He lifted his cup again. "Today, we drink to the Blood of *Quetzalcoatl*."

The mumbling crowd lifted their cups and joined in exaltation. "*Quetzalcoatl*!"

Six

The presidential office was dead silent except for the sound of Mario's boot tapping on the hard wood floors. He glanced at the Mexican flags, the antique brandy decanter and bar in the far corner of the room, then back at the *Presidente*.

Benito paced back and forth across the room for several minutes before settling at his desk. Perched regally in a high back leather chair with Mexican flags on each side of him, and a spectacular view of the *Zocalo* in the background, he quietly confided in him. "I loved your sister very much."

Angela mentioned Benito often. She seemed so happy ever since they found each other. Up until today, Mario assumed they would marry. "I know, *Senor Presidente*. She loved you too."

"Please call me Bene. Angel called me Bene."

"*Si, Senor Pres*—" He smiled for the first time since coming here. "I mean, *Bene*."

Bene sighed. "You have no idea how nice it is to be called by my first name. I have few real friends in this world, Mario, but I want us to become true *amigos*."

Under different circumstances, Mario expected to befriend his future brother-in-law at a dinner party, social event, maybe at his mother's house, but not like this. Besides, Bene already did so much for Mario without even knowing him. "*Gracias senor*, for recommending me for the job."

"You earned it."

Mario didn't know if he did or not. Men who worked entire lifetimes in government service never received such prestigious posts. He thought about taking Bene and Angela out to eat with his first paycheck. God apparently had other plans. He wanted to express these things to Benito, but didn't know where to begin.

Bene clenched his teeth. "Fate is cruel, Mario. For something like this to happen at your workplace, I feel terrible."

"It's not your fault, *senor*. Without your recommendation, I would never have been considered for the position since I've only been out of the military a month. Thank you."

"You were top of your class." Bene stared past him, his eyes glazed over. "Angela was so proud of you. She talked about you all the time."

A lump rose in Mario's throat. He gripped the arm of the chair, squeezed the armrest until it hurt, hoping to suppress his urge to cry. "*Si.*"

"We must find her killers. I would do it myself, but I am under such lock and key around here since the election, I can't even walk down the hall of this building without an escort anymore." Bene pounded his fists on the table. "We have to do something."

"*Si*, I agree." Mario hated to think of what he would do if he found the maniacs who tore his sister to shreds. He hoped the policia found them first so he could avoid breaking his mother's heart a second time with a jail sentence. "But what can we do, *senor*? I am nobody, you are somebody. The policia will handle it, correct?"

"I would like to think so, yes, but as you know, our government is not without corruption. Listen." Bene glanced over Mario's shoulder at the closed door leading to the hallway outside and lowered his voice. "I cannot be sure who I can trust. Whoever did this may try to kill me, some of my own Presidential guards might be enemies in disguise – I don't know. Even my own father…" He choked back tears. "These are dangerous times, *amigo*. I angered many people by getting elected."

Mario didn't say anything. He couldn't. He already knew Angela's murder probably had something to do with her new relationship with the controversial *Presidente*, and if he was honest with himself, he wasn't sure how he felt about it. Part of him wanted to be angry at Bene, punch him in the mouth right here and now, accuse him of murdering Angela himself, but he couldn't. Angela loved Bene too much, and to dishonor him in any way would diminish her memory. Plus, the man showed him nothing but kindness even before they met.

Angela recently told Mario all about Benito's miraculous rise to power, how the unknown Bene had no political experience and got elected solely by a group of eager marketers who capitalized on the name recognition of Mexico's first *Presidente*. Bullhorns and pickup trucks took to the streets and voters who never turned out to the polls before participated in electing the young man to office. Angela spoke passionately about Bene's election, how even the most illiterate of citizens recognized his name and turned out to vote. Many citizens were thrilled, even more were furious.

Bene tapped a pencil on his desk. "I caused Angela's death because of my enemies."

Mario gulped and tightened his grip on the chair. "No, *senor*."

A tear ran down Bene's cheek. "It's true, *amigo*. They wanted me, they got to her instead. I'm sure of it. I run it around in my mind, but I can't understand why. I can never live with myself until these barbarians are brought to justice. I'm afraid of what I will do to these people once I find them. I may be arrested, or killed myself. I don't care.

I must find Angela's killer in order to find any kind of peace in this life again."

Mario stared into the deep brown eyes of the young *Presidente* and realized they had much more in common than he originally thought. "What do you have in mind?"

Before he answered, two enormous men in plain grey business suits entered. Bene burst out of his seat. "Why are you interrupting?"

One man dropped a sealed manila envelope on the table. "*Senor Presidente*, we were informed to bring this to you right away."

The look on Bene's face made Mario feel queasy. *More bad news?* "What is it?"

Benito ran his finger along the edge of the envelope, hesitating before opening it. "I'm not sure we want to know." He spilled the contents on the table revealing a half a dozen grizzly crime scene photos he fanned out on the desk in front of him.

Mario caught a glimpse of Angela's lifeless body dangling on the stone altar. "Stop!" Without thinking, he leaned forward and covered the images with his forearms and elbows. "Don't look."

Bene sighed. "I need to see for myself."

Mario respected his wishes and backed away. The image would be burned in his own mind forever, with or without photographic evidence.

Bene's eyes filled with torment. "My God! What kind of monsters are these?"

Mario bowed his head and squeezed his hands together. "I don't know."

"This is unthinkable." He turned to his guard. "Who brought these?"

He shrugged. "We found them on the front desk, *senor*."

"Go and find out who put them there. Now."

Mario cleared his throat. "The body vanished by the time the *policia* arrived."

Bene gave Mario a knowing glance. They both knew the killers took the pictures. How they managed to deliver them to the *Presidente* with such ease and hide the body in broad daylight was another question. With the calm demeanor of a madman, Benito stacked the photos and slid them back into the envelope, stared into space for a second. "We need a plan."

"*Si*, we need a team, a group of your strongest men."

"No. Only you." Bene tapped the table and glanced around his office. "We need a meeting place where we are guaranteed privacy." He leaned closer. "I can't say for sure our conversation is safe even here."

"But where?"

Bene whispered in his ear.

Mario smiled. "*Si, muy bueno.*

Seven

Richard Ayala reclined in his high backed leather chair. Feet propped on his desk, he puffed on a cigar and enjoyed the view of the bright sunny day in the *Zocalo* down below.

Someone knocked.

He rolled his shoes off the credenza, tapped cigar ashes in an overflowing tray. "Come in."

One of his young male staff members walked in and tossed a manila envelope on his desk without a word. His suit clung to the muscles in his arms and legs, wisps of a jet black tattoo encircling his neck peeked up slightly around his collar.

Ayala shrugged. "*Que*?"

"Something you need to see, *Senor*."

Ayala opened the envelope, pulled the photos out, studied them carefully and nodded. "*Gracias*."

***

Across town, hundreds of well-dressed business people ascended a long flight of stone steps and reentered the hustle bustle of the *Zocalo* during the busiest time of day.

They laughed, joked around, exchanged niceties and business cards. Many congregated in local restaurants and received the best seats overlooking the *Plaza de la Constitucion*. They sipped ice cold tequila, discussed business matters and bragged on photos of their kids.

Far under the Catholic Cathedral Metropolitano, over a hundred mocha-colored hooded capes hung neatly on a wall of hooks until they would be needed again.

***

A busy executive sat behind his mahogany desk, reached for his brandy decanter, and poured himself a midday drink. His telephone rang at the precise moment he expected. "*Hola*?"

"*Senor*?"

"*Si*?"

"It is done."

"*Bueno*." The executive hung up the phone, lifted his glass and drank.

Eight

Mario shut the door to the Presidential chambers and walked alone down the constricted corridor stuffed with stern-faced guards who pointed the way out.

He didn't receive the presidential escort like before, instead, they directed him down the regular public staircase past dozens of guided tour groups where he exited like any other normal citizen – through the front door of the *palacio*.

Occasionally, he glanced over his shoulder and noticed the two thugs in business suits who interrupted his meeting with Bene followed a hundred or so feet behind. *Coincidence?* Maybe, although Bene didn't mention having him tailed. *Probably standard procedure, nothing to worry about.*

He walked faster and glanced back again once he reached the edge of the *Zocalo*. The men continued to follow. His gut said something wasn't quite right. He thought about calling Bene to check, but that was strictly against the rules they agreed on. Phone lines were easily tapped.

Mario refused to become paranoid. They were probably some of the Presidente's undercover officers who weren't doing a very good job of hiding themselves. Military training should have taught them better. Unless they wanted him to know they were watching, assuming he would find comfort or intimidation in the knowledge. He didn't. Mario had a feeling Bene wouldn't approve. From here on out, he could only trust Benito. Mario stepped outside into the hot sun and into the center of the *Zocalo's Plaza de la Constitucion*, where the Mexican people celebrated all facets of living. He shaded his eyes with his palm and gazed toward the other side of the square where the Mexican Supreme Court held session, and followed the line of shops until he got straight across from the Palacio, where an enormous shopping center, complete with hotels and restaurants, filled an entire city block. The thugs waited at the top of the stairs, right inside the *Palacio* doors, and when Mario turned around, they turned away to avoid eye contact. Now was his chance. He needed to ditch them soon for his plan with Bene to succeed.

First he had to go back next door and see about the investigation. The *Templo Mayor* was directly to his right, but he didn't want them to know his whereabouts, so he would need to do a few maneuvers first. If he ran across the busy city center to the other side, he might be able to get lost in the crowd and throw the two men off his trail. He glanced over his shoulder, and once they were busy talking to each other, he disappeared into the center of the *Zocalo* and went all the way to the other side without looking back. He slowed down near the shopping center, before ducking into a small clothing shop. When he turned back around, the men were nowhere in sight.

An elderly woman hunched over a cash register greeted him with a smile. "*Hola*."

"*Buenos dias*." Mario still wore his uniform from this morning, making him an easy target for anyone trying to find him. Stacks of gauze summer cotton pullovers folded neatly in the front corner of the store next to a pile of colorful blankets caught his eye. He thumbed through the shirts until he found his size. "*Cuanto*?" He reached for his wallet.

"*Cincuenta y cinco.*"

Fifty five pesos seemed steep for the flimsy shirt. He pulled fifty from his wallet and put it on the counter. "*Si?*"

The woman acted insulted and dramatically waved at the money. "*Cincuenta y cinco.*"

He shrugged to suggest he didn't have any more.

She placed the money in the drawer and reached for the shirt and a bag.

"No *gracias.*" Mario removed his uniform jacket and slipped the new shirt over his head. He glanced at his pants. *Beige, plain and unnoticeable. Good.*

The woman handed him a sack.

He stuffed his uniform jacket in the shopping bag and walked back out into the hot sun, glancing in both directions before putting on his sunglasses to further disguise himself.

He made a beeline across the *Zocalo* toward the Templo Mayor, hoping the *Presidente's* men would be gone by now. Outside the ruins, the line that normally stretched around the corner of the building at noon was nonexistent. Today a CLOSED sign and locked outer gates kept visitors away. Lupe went home for the day right after the policia arrived, so Mario walked around to the building in the back, which housed many of the Aztec wonders, and tried the door. Locked. He knocked with no answer and knocked louder again.

A large man who dressed like the Palacio guards let him in without ever asking to see his badge. Apparently the staff recognized him. Either that, or museum security was more lax than he realized. *Not good.* He stepped into the cool air conditioning.

The guard loomed over him. "Director wants to see you."

Mario followed him all the way to the back to the curator's office. He hadn't worked here long enough to know everybody's names, but he knew hers – Amelia Sanchez. Nice lady.

Sanchez was nowhere in sight. Instead, a short thin man in a grey plaid suit sat at her desk. His arms rested on a six inch high pile of papers. His nose covered most of his face and he stared at Mario with pinpoint eyes hidden behind layers of wrinkled skin and reading glasses. He held more copies of the grisly crime scene photos. "Mario Martinez?"

Mario wiped the sweat off his forehead. He never saw this man before and wondered if he could be trusted. "*Si.*"

He pointed to the chair closest to the door. "Take a seat."

Paranoia at an all time high, Mario glanced over his shoulder into the hall. "Where is Ms. Sanchez?"

The weird little man flipped through stacks of papers. "Running around here somewhere. I am the Director."

He extended his hand. "Mario Martinez. Nice to meet you."

The man kept his arms flat. "You met with *Senor Presidente* earlier?"

He nodded and kept quiet.

"Well?" He leaned back, folded his arms across his body. "What did the two of you discuss?"

Mario didn't want to get fired or risk betraying his confidence to Bene. This man was a stranger. "He heard about the murder, *senor.*"

The little man twisted his face in a knot. "I understand, but why would he talk to *you*, a low paid guard and call you *by name*?"

Mario inadvertently rubbed his palms off on the front of his pant legs, dropping his shopping bag to the floor. He reached over and picked it up. "Um..." Surely the man was kidding. The media loved the unmarried heartthrob and most eligible bachelor, Benito Juarez. They loved Mario's sister too. Her stunning features, long black hair and near-perfect face made her prime tabloid fodder. The paparazzi called her the future princess of Mexico and she may well have been if things were different. None of this was secret. The fact that Angela and Mario were siblings was perhaps less known, but wouldn't be for much longer.

The man peered over the top rim of his glasses. "Well?"

Mario's right leg quivered, so he kicked his foot around, pretended to shake off a cramp. "The victim, *senor*," he gulped. "...was my sister."

The man pulled a photo out of the stack, placed it on the desk and pointed "Her?"

The photo showed Angela Martinez walking in the *Zocalo* under an umbrella held by a masculine man with a beard. He touched the image. She looked radiant with Bene. He hoped to one day shake the horrific images of her broken body from his mind and remember her like this instead. "*Si.*"

The old man nodded. "Nothing else then?"

He lowered his eyes. "No, *Senor*."

He waved him out with a hand. "Very well. Go on. Take tomorrow off."

"*Si, gracias*." Mario felt the man's eyes pricking holes into the skin on his back as he turned and stepped into the hall. This would not be the end of the Director, he felt sure of it. Next time they met, he would not only know the man's name, but would be prepared with answers – ones he wanted the Director to hear.

Nine

For the rest of the afternoon, Bene stayed in his office with the door closed. He anxiously awaited his meeting with Mario and called every few minutes to get updates on the investigation, but so far, nothing new turned up.

He stared blankly at his computer monitor incapable of comprehending a single word he read. After awhile, he swiveled around in his chair and watched people walking in the *Zocalo* down below. Things appeared peaceful there today, but in reality, nothing could be further from the truth.

Surprisingly, media hadn't yet discovered the incident at Templo Mayor, which proved both blessing and curse. Media often shone a light on otherwise hidden corruption in the government and had an ongoing love affair with Benito. Reporters repeatedly sang his praises during the recent election and were undoubtedly a large reason why he now held the office of *Presidente*. As much as it pained him to admit, even to himself, Bene wished the paparazzi knew about Angela. They could help find her killers in ways he alone could not. With public opinion still on his side so soon after the election, the public outcry for justice might bring the killers to light.

Bene had high hopes for his new *amigo*, Mario. He hoped he hadn't put Angela's brother in grave danger by what they were about to do this afternoon. If all went well, he would stick to the current plan, if not, by tomorrow, he would tip the media himself. For now, he felt it would be best to wait and see what Mario discovered on his own without anyone else knowing about it.

A recent photo of his Angel sat on the far corner of his desk. He picked it up and ran his finger over her gorgeous face, trembling at the thought he would never see her again. Mario proved quite a kid, wise beyond his years. He noticed the family resemblance to his Angela. Dark wavy hair barely brushed his shoulders, high cheekbones, wide cocoa brown eyes, full mouth turned slightly downward from the heavy burden of his heart. Angela always smiled. He loved that about her. *Loved. Past tense.* He couldn't yet grasp the fact that her only brother Mario would be the closest he'd ever come to seeing his Angel ever again.

He put the picture back on the desk. Alone in his thoughts, he realized Mario was right. The two of them alone couldn't find Angela's killer. They needed help. Besides Mario, there were only three other men in the entire world who Bene trusted with his life. He picked up his phone. "Rita?"

"*Si?*" He listened while she lifted her phone off speaker and held it to her ear. "How are you? Need anything?"

Bene couldn't tell her he was falling apart. Not now. "Can you call the boys in here? Tell them to hurry." *The Boys* were Bene's childhood friends and classmates, Diego, Jorge and Ricardo. His father wisely decided they would make exceptional bodyguards for his son during his tenure in office. The Boys knew everything about Benito, and because he needed trusted advisors watching over him twenty-four-seven, nobody could do the job better than the friends he knew best.

He heard Rita scribbling on her pad. "*Si, Senor Presidente*. Anything else?"

"Yes, I need to go to Mass tonight and pray. Will you set that up, *por favor*?"

"*Si*, of course."

The more he thought about Mario, the more Bene realized he needed Angela's brother as an ally. "Also, I've been thinking. I want you to transfer someone to my staff effective immediately."

Rita's voice rose slightly. "Oh? Who?"

"Mario Martinez. He works at the—"

"Si, I know. *Angela's* brother." She had the same questioning tone he'd heard since childhood. Anytime he acted rashly, Rita always offered words of warning. "Are you sure?"

Funny how she could still make him feel like a child, even though he was the leader of Mexico now. "I know what I'm doing, Rita. One more thing. Keep this promotion to yourself. Martinez will be undercover."

Rita paused. "I won't tell anyone, Benito, but are you sure Mario's right for this position? He is awfully close to the case."

Bene clenched his jaw, tapped his pen on the desk. "Do I have your word?"

Rita sighed. "Of course."

"Not even my father. Also, if he calls or comes by, tell him I don't want to see him."

Obviously pained by this announcement, Rita groaned. "Mmm. *Si*."

Benito hung up the phone. He held Angela's picture. "Your brother and I will avenge you, my darling."

A few minutes later, someone knocked. Two of his three boys stood in the foyer blocking the light from the hall with their enormous frames. Thick muscles bulged from their matching grey suit jackets.

Bene glanced up from his computer. "Come in."

His friend Jorge removed his sunglasses and tucked them in his thick black hair. "You want to see us? If it's about Angela, I'm sorry, but we don't know anything yet."

Diego entered a split second behind him carrying a file which he plopped on Benito's desk. "We talked to the policia again a second ago. They took everything into evidence, but—"

Bene stood and moved around the desk to the conference table. "Si, close the door, take a seat." He peered into the hall, expecting to see his third guard. "Where's Ricardo?"

They remained standing, clasped their hands, bowed their heads. Diego pulled out a chair. "We have not seen him today, *senor*."

"Did you call him? Tell him about Angela?"

"We left a voicemail," Jorge said.

Bene rubbed his chin, glanced at his calendar. "Did he mention taking the day off?"

Jorge shook his head. "No *senor*. Not that I know of."

"Okay, well…a lot's happened today. I probably forgot."

Diego wrinkled his face. "What's this about, *senor*? Angela? Did you find something new?"

Bene pointed to the chairs across from him. "Sit down you two, and stop calling me *senor* for a minute. I need to talk to you about something important, as *amigos*." The two sat while Bene paced around his office. "I'm sure I don't need to tell you two we have a serious problem on our hands. Whoever did this to Angela—"

Diego ran his fingers over the holster of his gun. "Nobody will touch you, Benito. I swear on my life."

"What can we do to help you, *amigo*?" Jorge asked with concern in his eyes.

"What we discuss must stay between us, *comprende*?"

Both friends agreed. "Of course."

"Did you see the guard here earlier?"

Diego nodded. "The one you told us to follow earlier?"

Bene realized he should get Mario's photo taken for occasions like these. "*Si*. I asked you to follow him because I want him kept safe."

"We tried, but he ditched us," Jorge said.

Diego chuckled. "He actually did a pretty good job of it for about five minutes, until we caught him going inside *Templo Mayor*."

Bene normally found his friends amusing, but not today. "Stay on his trail, *comprende*?"

Jorge made sure to look Benito straight in the eye. "Don't worry. He showed up at *Templo Mayor* awhile ago, and we'll find him again once we leave here. His moves aren't hard to predict."

"*No problemo*." Diego agreed.

Bene hoped Mario's inexperience wouldn't be problematic. He needed to be patient with the young man. What bothered him more was the fact his other friend wasn't here. Surely Ricardo knew better than to take time off so soon after the election. "Did Ricardo go to *Templo Mayor* today?"

His friends both shrugged. "We don't know, boss. Haven't seen him."

"What's up with the guard?" Jorge asked.

Diego crossed his arms across his chest. "Yeah, why are you so worried about him?"

Bene cleared his throat. "He's Angela's brother."

The men's jaws dropped.

"He's going undercover at *Templo Mayor* to help find Angela's murderer. Only the five of us can know about this, *comprende*?"

"Anything you want, Bene," Jorge said.

"*Si*, it's done, brother," Diego agreed.

Bene felt more secure now. "Good. I knew you three would help."

Ten

After his visit with Curator Sanchez, Mario planned to look around the ruins one more time before his meeting with Benito later that day. Benito suggested they meet at the Cathedral Metropolitano. Clever idea, Mario had to give him that. Nobody would ever consider interrupting them in a holy place. Maybe before the meeting, some new information would turn up about Angela.

On his way out the front door of the museum, Mario noticed the same two *policia* officers from the morning whispering to themselves in a corner. "Did you find any leads on my sister's murder?"

The officers stopped talking when Mario came within earshot. The older man shook Mario's hand. "We scoured the area for blood and samples and sent them to the lab, other than that, nothing new to report yet. I'm sorry."

"We found this." The younger officer pulled out a gold heart necklace, sealed in a Ziploc bag and held it up.

Mario's heart quickened and he instinctually reached for the bag without thinking.

"Hey. Wait a moment." The officer pulled the Ziploc overhead and out of his reach. "This is evidence. We need to analyze this in the lab with the rest of the things we found, then the family can have it. This is a murder investigation, you know."

Mario withdrew his hand. "*Si*, I'm sorry, I—"

The older officer whipped out a pad of paper and began writing. "Do you know this necklace?"

"*Si*, I gave it to her for Christmas when we were kids."

Tucking the bag in the inner pocket of his uniform, the officer continued taking notes. "We need this for evidence, but I promise we will return it once the case is solved."

Mario didn't realize Angela still wore that silly thing. He assumed it would have been lost or tangled up in the bottom of her jewelry box after all these years. "Where did you find it?"

"Follow me." The older officer led him to the window where they could see out into the exhibit. "It was lying on the rock off to the right side over there. Probably fell off during the decapitation."

Mario backed away from the view, clutched his stomach. "I didn't need you to paint that picture for me."

The officer cleared his throat. "I'm sorry."

"*No problemo*. Just find the killers."

"We'll do our best, but as you know, in Mexico City we have plenty of other murders here today alone."

Mario didn't care about other people and the overburdened police department. The only thing on their side was Angela's relationship with Benito. Her high profile case would be considered worth the time and trouble to solve. Ironically the reason she was murdered would be the same reason her case would receive necessary attention and resources. Bene was right. Fate was cruel.

These officers obviously didn't realize Angela's involvement with *El Presidente*, but would find out soon enough. For now, it wasn't any of their business. He checked his watch. He needed to get home to see his mother and offered his hand to the older officer. "*Hasta luego*."

The officer handed him a business card. "Call with questions. We've got your number."

I'll bet they do.

***

Outside *Templo Mayor*, the summer heat wasn't the only thing making Mario feel ill. He still needed to go to his mother's house and break the news to her before she heard about Angela from someone else. For all he knew, the local news crew already broadcasted the murder all over Mexico City. God he hoped not.

He should have told her this morning, but knew his mother was still at work. He didn't want to ruin the last potentially good day of her life. He glanced at his watch. She wouldn't be off for a couple more hours. The next hour or two might be better spent looking around each hall in the *Museo* searching for clues. He turned around and went back inside.

Why would someone want to murder someone in such a horrific way? What did Angela do to deserve such a terrible end? Mario hoped to recover her body before going home to his mother. Telling Elsa Martinez about Angela's grisly murder would be bad enough without having to explain why her daughter's body vanished into thin air.

While he walked through the Museo, the scene from this morning's authentic Aztec sacrifice flashed in his mind like something out of one of his old high school textbooks. He never paid much attention to his Mexican history lessons, but after seeing exactly how the Aztecs performed ritual sacrifice, for the first time in his young life, he wished he'd listened better in school. If he had, it might help him catch the bastards who did this. He approached the ancient relics section realizing he needed to understand these items – how they worked, what they did - even better than the Director himself.

Filled to the rafters with Aztec treasures, *Templo Mayor* was divided into several sections, each depicting a different aspect of Aztec life. Mario went straight to the ritual sacrifice items. The *Museo* kept an enormous collection of implements used in human sacrifice – sacrificial altars, stone carved bowls used for holding blood and other vital organs, and hand shaped obsidian blades, used to cut the hearts out. Mario read the placards under each, trying to imagine how they were used, shivering at the thought of his sister's last moments on Earth.

One display contained a hand carved stone box used for storing the sacred heart. He recognized that from earlier. Another showcased a stone head with a blade sticking from the center of its skull. When he saw the blade, Mario realized he forgot to tell Bene about Angela's stolen head and heart. Probably for the best. Poor Benito seemed on the verge of collapse already without any more bad news. He made a note to tell him about it when he felt better.

He didn't know what to look for or where to begin. Yes, Angela was murdered with items like these, but it still didn't tell him why, or by whom.

Dim overhead lights illuminated the vestiges, the air conditioner always blasted on high to keep the items safe from decay, and provided a welcome relief from the summer sun outside. He walked down the spiral tile steps into the basement, wondering what they kept there, when he ran into the cleaning lady Rosa. She stood in the center of the tiled room and drained crimson water from her mop. "*Que pasa?*"

"Look," Rosa pointed her bony finger toward the roof.

The once white stucco ceiling popcorn fell to the floor, soaked with what appeared to be red paint. Mario realized this area sat directly under the Eagle Chamber. "Rosa, I think you should put that mop down, take a break and come with me until I can go find someone to fix this, okay?" He gently ushered the old woman over to a built in tile seat that ran along a far wall.

Rosa wobbled over to the bench mumbling about her desire to finish working. "Are you sure? I'm almost done."

He didn't want her destroying evidence, nor did he want the poor lady panicked. "No, Rosa. Please sit. Let me get you some water. Wait here, okay? I'll be right back." Mario ran up the steps to go get the *policia*. Although he didn't know much about forensic work yet, he knew enough to have the *policia* check and see if the red drippings were blood or paint.

***

Rosa sat on the bench and pulled a leftover cinnamon bun from her front pocket she kept from breakfast. She ate it carefully so as not to dislodge her false teeth.

The heavy sound of footsteps came out of the wall near the windows. Rosa hid the pastry behind her back.

One of the biggest men she'd ever seen walked through a wall and came toward her.

"*Hola.*" Rosa smiled but the stranger didn't reciprocate.

He looked angry. Not at her, per se, but he was clearly annoyed about something. She didn't think to make a sound when he lifted his arm. His intention didn't register in her mind until she saw the large grey stone in his hand.

Her mouth full of cinnamon bun, she didn't think to cry out for help. The man hit her right between the eyes. Her world went black.

* * *

Mario rushed up the stairs and called out to the same two officers who were standing in the main lobby of the Museo. "Hey, there's something down here you need to see."

"*Que?*" one of the *policia* asked.

"*Por favor*, come and take a look." Mario didn't want to explain after making a fool out of himself earlier this morning. They followed him down to the basement where he'd left Rosa only moments before. Despite his instructions, the old lady and her cleaning supplies vanished into thin air. Cold chills ran through Mario's body. Someone else knew about the bucket and must be watching. But from where? He didn't see anything out of the ordinary. He hoped she was okay. He noticed a few tiny drops of fresh red on the tile floor. *Not a good sign...* "Rosa? Rosa?"

Hands on his hips, the younger of the two officers seemed impatient. "What did you want to show us?"

"This." Mario glanced up at the dripping red ceiling tiles. "And this." He pointed to the fresh spot of red on the floor near the bench. "The cleaning lady showed this to me and I told her to wait here. This red spot wasn't here when I called you two down here."

The younger officer rolled his eyes. "Uh huh."

"I swear," Mario pleaded.

"She probably took a break," one officer said.

"Is there another way she could have gotten out?" the older officer asked.

To his right, Mario noticed two double doors led to a restricted area. He walked up and tried them. No luck. *Later I will investigate.* For now, he decided it might be too dangerous. Mario shook his head. "Locked."

"We'll look into this later," the older officer said. "We can check it in the lab and see if the sample is consistent with the crime scene."

"Crime scene? I thought you said I made the whole thing up," Mario said.

The older officer lowered his eyes, sighed. "No, I'm afraid we found the blood evidence to back up your story. That and the fingerprints tell us you're right. Angela Martinez was murdered this morning. Now we'll work to recover the body, or at least try and figure out what happened down there."

Mario's brain turned to mush. He didn't hear anything but mumbling after the declaration that Angela Martinez was murdered. His hands shook uncontrollably. Being vindicated as a reliable witness would feel good in any other circumstances, but now, hearing this…He couldn't believe it was true.

"You know something?" The younger officer pointed to Mario and raised his eyebrows. "The only common denominator in any of this is you. Sure you don't have something you want to tell us, Martinez?"

Mario's jaw and fist tightened. If not for his military training, pure instinct would drive him to send the officer to the floor. Instead, he took a deep breath, counted to three.

Jerks always wanted to pick fights and in order to keep good military standing, soldiers were trained to let things roll off their shoulders. Keeping his cool today was particularly tough. He never felt so insulted. "You better watch yourself. That's my sister you're talking about."

The officer shrugged. "Hey, I'm just saying every time we pull up blood samples like these, you're alone in the area, all by your lonesome. A bit strange if you ask me…"

Mario lunged at the young policeman, pulled his fist back, about to crack his jaw in two, when heavy hands held him back.

"Hold on now you two." The older officer pulled Mario out of range and scolded his partner. "That's no way to talk to a man who just lost a sister. We're still investigating things." He swung Mario around, patted his shoulders. "Why don't you go on home? We've got it covered for now and tomorrow we'll all be fresh."

"I'll never feel better," Mario yelled. "My sister is dead and you two need to help me find the killers without accusing me of being the problem."

The older officer spun him around facing the stairs. "Calm down. You don't need to be hanging around here anymore. I'm sure your family needs you right now."

Family. Yeah right. His mother would be much harder to deal with than this.

Eleven

The peaceful sounds of chanting filled the air of the legendary Cathedral Metropolitano as Archbishop Salazar made his afternoon rounds.

The Cathedral served as the main worship site for the people of Mexico City, and the sacred ground on which the temple Ruins were found buried deep beneath church property.

Legend said the Aztec god of creation *Quetzalcoatl* was born at this very location and for hundreds of years the site was used for ritualistic purposes.

The church was built starting in 1573 over a period of two hundred and fifty years, which accounts for the strange architecture throughout the structure. The early Catholics were eager to stamp out any forms of paganism amongst local tribes, so they dismantled what they could of the temple complex, buried the rest, and actually used the same exact brick to construct their own place of worship.

In the ancient times of *Huitzilopochtli*, Aztec legend told about a powerful stone idol removed from its sacred resting place on top of the pyramid of Tenochtitlan under the watchful eyes of Cortes himself. The gods entrusted the idol to a man called *Tlatolatl* for safekeeping. Only Bishop Juan Zummaraga saw the idol since then, during his investigation of the matter in 1530, shortly before his death. Scholars speculated the carving was hidden away deep in the mountains of northern Mexico.

Current Cathedral Metropolitano Archbishop, Juan Zummaranga Salazar was the ancestral product of the wayward priest's torrid love affair with a priory nun. Nobody knew this about the good Father, or at least nobody dared to question his rise to the most powerful position in the church. Lost in his own thoughts, Salazar stood next to the chancel listening to the choir. He checked his watch and his way to the confessional. Slipping inside the wooden box, he heard the sound of breathing. "*Buenos dias*."

A woman whispered from behind the wooden blockade. "Bless me Father, for I have sinned."

Salazar listened attentively for the next forty five minutes, while the woman gave her un-extraordinary account of her sinful life since her last confession, including selfishly taking an extra portion of food at a family meal. He spoke through the wooden grate. "You are forgiven."

"Bless you, Father." The woman left with new lightness in her heart.

A nun approached Salazar as he walked toward the church office. "Father, *El Presidente* would like to use the Cathedral at 4:30 this afternoon for private worship."

"Would he like to confess or take Communion?" Salazar asked.

"No Father," the tiny nun said. "He wants to participate in Mass at 5:00 p.m., but he first would like to be alone for spiritual reflection."

"Fine. Notify the others to retire to remain in their quarters until five and call *Senor Presidente's* secretary to confirm."

She bowed. "Yes, Father."
***

Ricardo Hidalgo dabbed the bandages covering the fresh tattoo around his neck and walked to the parking lot to get into his car when his cell rang. He glanced at the caller ID and saw his old friend calling. "*Hola?*"

"Ricardo, where have you been?" Diego sounded concerned.

He didn't have time to deal with this. "Why? What's up?"

"Benito needs us to meet him at Cathedral Metropolitano at 4:00p.m. today."

The clock was ticking. He had much to prepare. "What? You and Jorge can't handle Benito by yourselves? Come on, man."

"He's got special instructions, *amigo*." Diego paused. "Angela...she's been murdered."

Ricardo tried to sound surprised. "Oh."

"Long story. Look, I don't want to talk about it on the phone, but Benito seemed pretty upset you weren't at work today. You didn't tell us what was up, bro, so it was kinda hard to have your back. Just get over here, *comprende*?"

Ricardo realized this situation might be to his advantage if he played it right. "What exactly does he need us to do?"

Diego sighed. "There's another undercover guy who Benito brought in to help solve the murder. He wants us to make sure he doesn't have any problems, if you get what I'm saying."

This could be bad. Benito never compromised on his private security. "Who's the guy?"

"His name is Martinez."

Ricardo smiled. "*Martinez*?"

"Si, Mario Martinez. Angela's brother. Think you can get there a little early and let him in?"

Things were working out better than Ricardo could ever imagine. "*Si*, of course. I'll be there."

"You better be. We'll bring Benito with us."

"I said I'll be there and I will." He hung up the phone and sat in the parking lot, stared at the steering wheel of his car. This stroke of luck might be the big break Ricardo needed to rise in the ranks of his organization. He scrolled through the numbers in his phone and dialed.

A deep voice answered. "*Hola*?"

Ricardo cleared his throat. "Um yes, sir? I think I found a way for us to fulfill our mission."

"Who is this?"

"Ricardo Hidalgo. I'm a personal body guard for *El Presidente* Benito Juarez."

"Tell me more…"

Twelve

Still fuming when he left *Templo Mayor*, Mario couldn't believe the officer actually accused him of killing his sister and causing Rosa's disappearance. He had a funny feeling in his gut about Rosa. The *policia* too. He remembered what Benito said about trust. He hoped those officers were trustworthy. Better to play it safe for now. He planned to meet Bene in just minutes and would discuss this with him then.

When Mario arrived at the Cathedral Metropolitano the *Zocalo* was still packed with people. He followed Benito's instructions and walked around to the very back door where a dark red awning hung above the priest's entrance. He held his breath, wondering if he could pull off such an elaborate stunt. Normally he would think twice about such a mission, but with Angela dead and her killers still on the loose, he would do whatever it took, regardless of the danger involved.

He trusted Bene's judgment although if anyone saw him, there would be hell to pay in this life and the next. Impersonating a priest must be a mortal sin, but right now that didn't matter. He grabbed the door handle and was about to go inside the Cathedral when one of the big suited thugs who followed him from Benito's office appeared from around the corner. Mario nearly jumped out of his skin. He wondered if he should abandon the mission right there and then, or keep on going. "Uh…*hola*."

Well over six feet tall, the man wore the same grey business suit he had on earlier that afternoon. Sunglasses hid his dark eyes and facial features. "Martinez?"

Mario wondered why he was here. Benito gave the impression only the two of them knew about their meeting. He stared at the man, gulped.

"Listen," the thug whispered. "Bene asked me to make sure you get in here okay." A thin line of blood soaked through the collar of the man's white dress shirt.

Mario noticed a fresh barbed wire tattoo encircled his neck. Didn't he see something like that earlier? Yes, but where? Ah yes, the subway. One of those boys had a similar tattoo, didn't he? Yes, Mario felt sure of it. But why was this man here? *Strange.* Either Benito told him about the meeting or his office really was bugged.

The giant stepped closer and loomed over him. "You are Mario Martinez, *si*?"

Should he pretend otherwise? No. He would be positive and trust. "*Si.*"

Obviously sensing Mario's uneasiness, the man assumed a more relaxed posture. "I'm one of Bene's friends from school. I'm also his guard. He didn't think you could get in here today without me. No big deal, *comprende*?"

"*Si.*"

The thug opened the door with a key, and Mario followed him down a short hall to a dressing room. "The robes are in there. You wait until exactly 4:31p.m, then go into the confessional, okay? Once we come get Bene, wait until you hear us exit and then come straight back here, change back into your street clothes and get out. Remember, wait until we leave. It's important." Without another word, he turned and disappeared.

Mario didn't like any of this, but what could he do? He could Benito's office just to make sure, but what good would that do? *El Presidente* would be here in a minute, besides, the phones were probably bugged.

He walked inside the small room. A single window provided some light to the changing area behind a solid oak partition. Several red and gold robes hung side by side on hooks. Mario felt strange putting them on. Ever since childhood, he went to Catholic Church and always believed priestly garments to be Holy. He hoped he wouldn't burn in Hell for this. He pushed those thoughts from his mind and sifted through the robes until he found one that looked about his size. He slipped it on over his head, sat behind the partition and waited, listened for any sign of noise outside the door. He heard nothing. Silence.

His pulse pounded in his temples. Several minutes passed when he heard the door to his room open and footsteps. Someone stepped inside. He peeked between the cracks of his hiding space and saw Father Salazar literally inches away. *Oh my God!* Mario held his breath. He cringed thinking what might happen if Salazar discovered him back here. With or without Bene's guards protecting him, it would be a disaster.

Before panic overtook him, the priest walked out and closed the door. Mario breathed a sigh of relief. He hunched behind the partition, his hands in prayer and asked the higher power to look out for him and Bene today. God knew they needed all the help they could get. Once this meeting finished, he would tell Benito to find another place to meet – a park, a shopping center, anything but this.

Thirteen

At 4:15p.m., the Presidente's guards approached the Cathedral Metropolitano. Ricardo slipped through the door and noticed Jorge and Diego asking tourists and worshippers to exit.

Jorge saw him immediately and walked over, slapped his old friend on the back. "Hey, Ricardo. Where've you been today? Bene asked about you."

The wound on Ricardo's neck stung. He gently pulled his collar away from his skin, loosened his black tie. "Yeah, sorry man. Family business."

Diego approached. "Hey you two. We only have a few minutes to scan this whole place." He tapped Ricardo on the shoulder. "And what about you? You took care of our man Martinez?"

If you only knew... Ricardo smiled. "*Si.*"

Jorge took a step closer and leaned forward. "Hey man, you're bleeding."

Ricardo lifted his fingers to his neck and dabbed the wound. "Yeah, it's nothing."

Diego pointed to the thick black lines. "Did you get another tattoo?"

Ricardo scowled and ignored him. "Let's get moving."

The three friends worked together for so long, they silently followed protocol, scouring every corner, rubbing their fingers under each pew, checking diligently for any recording devices, bugs or bombs. They opened all the closed doors, checking for unexpected surprises, each man assigned to his specific area of the Cathedral. Once everything appeared clear, the men met in front of the altar and gave the signal to the guards outside for Benito to enter.

At exactly 4:30 p.m. sharp, under heavy guard, the *Presidente* arrived. His head hung low, covered by a piece of beige gauze to disguise his identity from onlookers outside. Bene's entourage led him through the rear entrance of the Cathedral. His second tier bodyguards normally performed a routine scan of the church after The Boys, but today, they took extra precaution, sweeping every nook and cranny twice, and then again a third time, before finally releasing him to the privacy of the confessional in the back. With Benito in the care of his most trusted friends, the second tier guards went outside, where they would keep close watch on the church perimeter for the duration of the presidential visit.

Jorge approached. "All clear, *Senor Presidente*."
***

"*Muchos gracias.*" Bene shook Jorge's hand, smiled at Ricardo and Diego, and walked toward the confessional.

Earlier, his friends tried to dissuade him from coming here today, but he refused to listen. He had multiple reasons to visit this Holy site this afternoon, although he appreciated their concern, and felt relieved knowing they had his back in this dark time of need.

Bene slipped inside the same confessional booth he always used. Like a familiar friend, he welcomed the opportunity to unburden his soul, even to Mario Martinez.

Bene closed the confessional door, took a seat on the wooden bench, and waited for the one inch crack to appear in the sliding window between his stall and the other. He saw the flash of red and gold silk and waited until he heard the door close. "Bless me Father, for I have sinned."

Fortunately a familiar voice answered. "Yes, you have, and what will you do about it?"

Bene cleared his throat and whispered. "Mario?"

"*Sí*."

"You made it inside okay?"

"*Sí*."

Bene sighed with relief. "Good. Tell me, my brother, what did you learn today?"

Mario briefly described the crime scene when he first found it, the missing head and heart and the cleaning lady with the bloody mess downstairs. "When I brought the *policia* downstairs to question Rosa and to collect the mop and other evidence, she disappeared. Fresh blood on the bench suggests—"

Bene's gut tightened. "You believe they got her too?"

"I don't know. I hope not, but the woman is old and senile and couldn't move very well, but she and her supplies vanished within seconds."

"It does sound suspicious," Bene said.

"*Si*, plus I felt like someone was watching me. I didn't know what to do, *senor*. I didn't want to tell the *policia* since we don't know who we can trust, but I did anyway, in case something actually happened to Rosa."

Benito clasped his hands in prayer. "You did the right thing telling them, Mario."

"Did I? I've thought about calling you several times today to ask what you want me to do—"

"No Mario," Bene said. "Trust your instincts. That's what makes you the top of your class."

"*Si, senor*, but you are *El Presidente*—"

Benito appreciated Mario's conscientious work ethic and his naiveté. "I trust you, Mario. Whatever you think is best, do that and know you have my blessings."

They sat in silence for a few moments. Bene checked his watch. This session could not go any longer than his other confessions or else it might arouse suspicions. The facade of normalcy must be kept intact.

Bene prayed every single day since his presidency began a little over a month ago. Normally he asked God to intervene in the wellbeing of Mexico, end suffering of his people, or for his ability to use sound judgment. Always with a somber but willing heart, he prayed, but today, his heart was broken. "We must continue to meet here while you work undercover at the *Museo*. I do not want any suspicion aroused."

He heard Mario sigh. "I don't know, Bene. Father Salazar almost caught me. I'm not sure this is a good idea. There must be a better place. A park, a mall..."

"No Mario. I told you. In any of those places, I am on public display. We must meet here."

"Okay. I can be off work by this time every day. Will this work for you?"

"Si, I will make due until we find out who wants me dead."

"I hope that is not the case, *senor*."

Bene hoped it wasn't true either, but the fact that someone murdered his Angela meant his enemies were circling and could strike at any moment. "I wish they'd asked for ransom, or votes, money, anything, but to take my Angel from me and not give me a chance to save her..." He broke down in tears.

Fourteen

Mario was just about to ask Bene about the man who met him at the door earlier, but when he heard the sound of Bene sobbing, he stopped himself. He was angry Bene violated their confidence by asking his friend to come here, but now was not the time to discuss it. Besides, Benito probably had his reasons.

Bene sniffed and blew his nose. "I would give my life for your sister. I must find her killer."

Mario leaned his forehead in his hands. "I know. Believe me, I know. I spent the whole day at the *Museo* trying to figure out who did this. I met the Director—"

"Dennis Montoya?"

"I don't know. He never introduced himself to me."

"Small eyes, big nose?"

"*Si.*"

"*Si*, that's Montoya. What did he want?"

Mario leaned closer to the window and spoke softly. "He seemed very interested in why you called me for a private meeting and showed me a photo of you and Angela walking across the *Zocalo* in the rain. I didn't tell him anything. Just that you were worried about me because she was my sister."

Bene sighed so loudly, Mario could hear it from his booth. "I remember that time. Angel looked so beautiful, so perfect..." He broke down again.

Mario knew he had to bring up a sensitive topic Bene probably hated discussing with Angela. "What about her new job?"

Bene didn't say a word at first. "With *Partido La Gente*?"

"*Si*, don't you think those people might like to see you dead?"

"Oh I don't know. We view politics very differently and have conflicting ideas about what is best for Mexico and rarely see eye to eye, but surely that is no cause for—"

Mario cleared his throat. "Benito, *senor*, no disrespect, but I believe you may be overlooking the dangers. The newspapers reported your own party is angry at you for dating Angela because she works for them I mean *worked.*"

"I know, but there must be more to it than that."

"Have you considered this might be a political move designed as an Aztec ritual to throw us off the trail?"

"I haven't had much time to think of everyone who may or may not want to hurt us, but I suppose it makes sense.

Angela was so happy when she landed that job. The people's party leaders recognized her work with the homeless, loved her writing and her attitudes. She finally felt like she'd received recognition as a writer."

Mario nearly choked listening to Bene. This topic caused much strife in the Martinez household. He personally hated the fact his sister left her long running position with the established city newspaper to join the radical political party, but not half as much as their mother did. After penning a few controversial articles, Angela won over the party leader Ayala who was considered by some to be nothing short of a terrorist. "I never approved, Bene. I still don't. Those people are no good. Did she say anything to you about any stories she was working on?"

"No."

"What if she got in over her head?"

"Possible..."

"What if she knew something?"

" *Si*, anything is possible. I've been too upset today to think about it, but I will."

Mario felt sick. He had a bad feeling they were involved somehow. "I will check them out during my lunch hour tomorrow."

"Be careful," Bene warned.

"I will. You too." Mario heard a loud knock on Benito's side of the booth and the sound of someone whispering.

"It's time," Bene said. "They're telling me I have to go now."

"Until tomorrow." Mario followed instructions and waited. He listened to the sounds of Bene's door slide open, his footfall on the floor joined with several other pairs of feet, until the sound of him and his guards faded off into the distance. *So far so good.* He kept his head bowed and slipped out of the confessional, hoping to make it back to the changing area and exit before anyone stopped him.

"Father?"

Mario glanced over his left shoulder and saw the Archbishop Father Salazar. He wanted to run, but if he and Bene were going to meet here daily, Mario knew he would need to face Salazar eventually. He could not hide in the changing room forever. Better this happen now so he could rid himself of his fear of running into the legendary priest. Bene's guard would not be happy about it if he ever found out though. "Father Salazar, so nice to see you." Mario clasped his hands in prayer, bowed.

Salazar looked him over. "Father Martinez, I must say I was surprised to hear *El Presidente* requested you to conduct his daily Confession today. I've worked with him and his father for years now."

Mario had to pull this off. He swallowed hard and tried to remain calm. "Oh well, I don't think it is any reflection on you, Father Salazar. *Senor Presidente* tells me you are a wonderful counselor and trusted spiritual guide."

Salazar scratched his chin. "How do you know Benito?"

Mario hadn't figured that part of the story out yet. "We went to church together many years ago."

Salazar smiled. "Oh? In *Districto Federal*?"

Mario agreed because he didn't know what else to say. "Uh, *si*."

Salazar nodded. "Very nice there…"

"*Si*. Good day, Father." Mario bowed and turned to go.
***

Father Salazar watched with great interest as the supposed Father Martinez walked away. He resented Benito meeting political people in a house of worship, especially since the young *Presidente* didn't bother to train his undercover agents on his background as a farmer's son. "Districto Federal," Salazar laughed to himself. Even now as *Presidente*, Benito's salary would not sustain that neighborhood, and probably never could.

Salazar stepped into a smaller chapel in the back of the building and prepared to say private Mass for Benito. He carefully laid out the Holy Water, bread and wine, lit the candles.

He peeked into the sanctuary where Bene normally waited, surprised he was nowhere to be found. "Benito?" Salazar stepped into the hallway and walked past the long bank of confessionals. The church was completely empty. "*Senor Presidente*? Benito?"

Fifteen

Jorge and Diego walked ahead to clear the path for Ricardo and Bene to exit the Cathedral. The three friends followed the same exact routine whenever *El Presidente* attended Mass. Ricardo counted on the other guards staying at the front and back sides of the church. The alleyway always remained empty so Benito could leave uninterrupted.

Just before he stepped outside, Ricardo turned to Bene. "Today we're doing things a little differently. Stand inside the door and wait until I come get you. We want to take extra precautions, just in case."

"Good idea, *gracias*." Bene never questioned any decisions his boys made.

Ricardo stepped into the alley outside where his two friends waited and closed the door behind him.

"Hey," Jorge said. "Where's Bene?"

At that moment, a tall lanky young man walked around the corner, providing a necessary distraction. The kid grabbed Diego and held him down.

"Hey." Jorge started to lunge at the kid when Ricardo pulled a switchblade and slit his throat. Jorge collapsed on the concrete before he knew what hit him.

"Ricardo?" Diego cried in disbelief. "What are you doing?"

"A man's gotta do what a man's gotta do." Ricardo grinned, lunged forward and slit Diego's throat, tossing him on top of Jorge's lifeless body.

"Now what?" the tall kid asked.

"You want to earn your keep?"

"*Si.*"

"Then you do this." Ricardo sunk the knife into Diego's chest cavity with all his might, tore his torso open and cut out his heart. "Give me the box."

The young man removed a stone box out of the canvas sack on his shoulder, handed it over to Ricardo with a shaking hand.

"Put his heart in here, seal it like this…" Ricardo wrapped the box several times with a sinewy twine. "There… now you try." He held his hand out, offered his knife and pointed to Jorge.

The boy took the knife. His hand shook like a leaf. "I…don't know if—"

"Ah. Give me that. There's no time to waste." Ricardo repeated the performance on Jorge's corpse. "Now hand me the box."

"Uh," the kid stammered. "I only brought one."

Ricardo rolled his eyes. "Fine." He handed the heart to the kid. "Hold this."

Despite his role in the killings, the kid seemed repulsed by the bloody mess. "What am I supposed to do with it?"

"Wait here. I'll tell you in a minute." Ricardo opened the door and went inside to get Bene.

***

Bene stood inside the Cathedral door wondering what was taking so long. He expected to attend Mass tonight with Father Salazar, but apparently with all that happened today Rita must have made other arrangements for security purposes. He checked his watch, tapped his shoe on the stone floor.

When the outer door finally opened, Ricardo stood before him, covered in blood. Bene's pulse quickened, his stomach knotted up. "Ricardo. What's going on? Are you okay?"

Ricardo grabbed him by the arm and held him so tight, he couldn't move. "Fine. Come on."

Just outside the door, Bene saw the horrifying sight of his best friends lying dead in the alley. "Oh my God. Who did this?" Before Bene fully comprehended what happened, Ricardo punched him in the stomach. He doubled over and felt someone slip a bag over his head. A sharp pain stabbed the back of his skull. His world went black.

Sixteen

S lipping out the back entrance to the Cathedral wearing his new street clothes, Mario felt like a complete idiot for not being better prepared to face Salazar. He should have known the priest would eventually approach him and been more prepared. Having Benito replace him in the confessional must have been quite a bruise to the older priest's ego. Mario made a mental note to ask Bene about his time at Districto Federal. Perhaps Bene could call the priest and tell him Mario would be coming so the next time he ran into Salazar things would be less awkward.

Outside the afternoon sun blared down on the streets. Mario put his sunglasses back on and took a look around. So far, so good, although he realized he could never be too sure whether or not he was followed. The alleyway behind the Cathedral offered adequate cover, at least for now. He walked several blocks toward the *Paseo de la Reforma*. Hundreds of plastic tarps lining the streets served as makeshift homes for thousands of people. He couldn't help but think of his sister when he saw the homeless, because in life Angela was a major champion for their cause. He stood on a corner for a second, watching a couple of men fry an egg in small pan under their tent. They split it between them and greedily devoured the small portion. Angela would often buy food from restaurants and pass it down the lines here. What would they do without her? Mario still couldn't believe she was gone.

He dipped into one of the many metro stations and boarded a train. Tonight instead of going straight home, he needed to complete the unfortunate task of breaking the news to his mother. The weight of this burden weighed heavily on him all day long.

He sat in a back corner pressed against a window while the train zipped out of the station. Dozens more people crammed into the tiny space with each subsequent stop. Mario closed his eyes, gritted his teeth together, wondering if he had the strength or the words for his mother. He should have called her earlier, or left the city altogether this afternoon, but he hadn't felt up to it, and still didn't. He could always use Bene as the excuse, but he made the decision to stay downtown. He wasn't man enough to face his own mother and tell her Angela was never coming home. He'd rather face a firing squad at close range than this. Justifications rolled through his mind. Bene needed him, he was detained and working at the Museo. None of these were excusable, but an hour or two would not make a difference in the grand scheme of things. Their lives were ruined this morning and things would never be right again.

He tried to imagine how his mother would react. He played the scene over in his mind, as much for his own benefit as hers. He wanted to be prepared even though nothing could get him ready for such a horrific confession. The news might kill her. In one scenario, he imagined her falling down and convulsing in full cardiac arrest. Did he remember CPR? He thought so, although he only practiced in class, never on a real person. He ran over the steps in his mind, just in case. Tilting the head back, pressing the chest, pausing, breathing into the mouth with the nose plugged. Yes. If she fell down, he could offer her medical assistance. He pulled his cell from his pocket, made sure the battery was charged in case he needed to call for emergency help.

God how he hated to bear such horrific news! In all his days he dreaded this situation more than any other. Mario went through tough times in his life, but this would be the worst he ever endured.

He rode until the train cleared of most passengers and exited at the end of the line in the overcrowded northern part of Mexico City. A short walk from the station brought him to his family home, a modest two bedroom flat with a corrugated tin roof crammed atop a once majestic mountain, along with hundreds of other houses. He walked these roads a thousand times as a child, but today he could barely make it up the hill without losing his breath. Visions of Angela walking him to school filled his mind. She always watched out for him. Not anymore.

Standing on the gravel leading up to the front door, Mario saw the lights on in the kitchen and smelled something wonderful through the windows. He held his breath and moved forward slowly and finally knocked.

His mother called out and within a second, she swung the door open, her plump figure hidden behind a stained apron. She waved the wooden spoon in her hand. "*Que pasa*? I didn't know you were coming for dinner today, but lucky I made your favorite *menudo*. Come in. Your sister came by yesterday so there's still some leftover *flan*, and my *tamales* are…" She stopped suddenly, stared at her son who still stood outside on the porch. "Mario?" She put her hands on her hips. "What's wrong?"

Even though he played this moment again and again in his mind, seeing his mother standing there in front of him proved more difficult than he realized. Mario told himself he'd be strong, but looking into the kind eyes of the woman who loved him, he couldn't hide his emotions. His face tightened. A tear popped out of his right eye. He gulped, tried to speak.

"Mario?" His mother put her wooden spoon down on the counter, untied her apron and tossed it over an old torn up chair they had in the family ever since he could remember. She put her arm around his shoulder and shook him. "Mario? *Que pasa*?"

Tears spilled over his cheeks, his legs buckled. "Mama…" He grabbed her shoulders and shook her, then let go and sat down on the chair, hiding his eyes in his hands. "Oh Mama…"

"*Que*?" She walked over and sat on an end table, not bothering to remove the stacks of old newspapers piled too high. "Did you get fired?"

He shook his head. He wished. That would be easy compared to this. "No."

"Well then what?"

He had to be a man and tell her now. He couldn't wait and have her wondering why her daughter wouldn't return her calls or show up to finish her favorite *flan*. "Something happened today, Mama."

The look on his mother's face would be burned in Mario's mind the rest of his life. Her lip began quivering in anticipation of bad news. "*Que*?"

"Angela…" He broke down. "Angela…"

Her eyes wide, she stood up and yelled. "Is she hurt? Where is she? " She shook Mario's shoulders, but when he didn't respond, she walked to the kitchen window and peered into the yard outside, expecting Angela to walk up the steps any moment.

Mario stood and walked to her, put his arms around her shoulders and tried to pull her away from the window. "She's not coming, Mama."

His mother turned around and cried. "Why not? What happened?"

Mario stared into her eyes. "Angela is dead, Mama. Murdered."

He watched her fear of the unknown fade while the horror of his words seeped into her consciousness. He knew those looks, those feelings. They were the same he had around nine this morning. She searched his eyes, hoping to find a new answer hidden somewhere inside him. Her hands trembled. "When?"

"This morning, last night maybe."

Without warning, his mother slapped him hard across the face. "And you just now told me?"

Mario didn't even try to ease the pain of his stinging face. He deserved it. She was right. There was no excuse for him not coming here earlier. He helped his mother to a chair. "Sit, *por favor*."

Elsa leaned into the chair and pressed her palms against her thick legs which started to shake. Her face twisted in a knot, lips pursed, eyes watered. "No. This cannot be. This isn't true." She leaned forward, pounded her fists against Mario's legs. "Please. Tell me this isn't so."

Mario cradled her in his arms like she did for him when he was a baby, rocked her back and forth. "I wish I could, but I can't."

She howled. "No!"

Mario rubbed her back and rocked her until he felt her let go.

Finally, only a few sniffles remained. "How?"

He didn't want to answer this question. *Did she really need to know?* "I found her at *Templo Mayor* this morning."

His mother scowled. "Why didn't you come tell me?"

Mario wasn't sure he wanted to bring up Benito just yet. His mother always felt uneasy about Angela dating him. "Because I am helping the investigation."

"Where is she? Where's the body? In the morgue? I want to see her." She frantically got up and grabbed her purse and keys. "I need to see my baby."

Mario wrung his hands together and wondered how his mother would ever rest knowing her daughter's mutilated body disappeared. "That isn't possible, Mama."

"Why not?" She slammed her purse on the table. "*Por favor.* Take me to her now."

Mario pulled the keys from her fingers and tried to get her back into the chair. "I can't. Somebody murdered her and left her in the Eagle Chamber. I've been working all day with the policia to try and find answers, Mama, but—"

His mother's eyes grew wide and without Mario having to describe the scene at all, it seemed she knew already. She pushed him away. "This was Bene Juarez' fault. This was *Partido La Gente's* fault. If she stayed with the paper, met a normal man, she would still be alive." She threw stacks of newspapers filled with Angela's articles across the room. They hit the wall, sending several porcelain figures crashing to the floor. "Bene Juarez did this to her. I warned her. She wouldn't listen."

Mario honestly couldn't say he disagreed with his mother's position, but these hateful words could never bring his sister back now. "No, Mama."

She pointed a shaking finger at him. "*Sí*. It's true. You know it. You warned her too."

Mario closed his eyes and put his head in his hands. He wished this would go away, but until he could get justice and closure for Angela, he knew it never would. He never liked her job either, but this discussion was too little too late. Nothing would bring her back.

His mother stood at her door with her keys in her hand. "I want you to take me to my daughter right now."

He grabbed his mother's shoulders and held her in his hands. "Listen. That is not possible. Please. Do not make me tell you more right now. When you can see her, you will, okay? Stop. Please. Trust me."

She sobbed and collapsed in his arms. "Okay."

Mario would pray every moment of his remaining time on Earth that he could find his sister's body and bring her back to their mother so she could provide a proper burial for her. He knew Elsa was both strong and stubborn and soon he would have to tell her the whole story. He hoped by then to find Angela's body so she could rest in peace.

Seventeen

Juarez Senior paced in the living room of his one story home, sipped tequila and stared out the window. Normally this time of night he and his son shared a drink and light conversation, but Bene hadn't called or spoken to him since this morning.

He picked up the phone, dialed Bene's private hotline number for the sixth or seventh time. No answer. He hung up and stared out the window into the yard. He regretted the words between them this morning. He hated Angela died, but in some ways, getting the radical out of the picture would be the best thing to happen to Bene's presidency since it began. Angela threatened to undo all the work and effort to get him elected, but with her out of the picture, hope for Benito's political future returned.

He understood his son's outrage, but to yell at his own father in front of his entire staff? Benito's actions were totally uncalled for and humiliating. The cabinet members would soon forget the incident, Bene would eventually recover from his grief, just like he'd gotten over all the other wrong women Juarez steered him away from through the years. Life would go on. Fine. But to miss their evening drink? This seemed exceptionally harsh punishment, even for Bene. He called two other numbers and both went straight to voicemail. Finally, he tried the only other person who might know Bene's whereabouts.

The phone rang twice and Rita picked up. "*Si*? *Senor* Juarez?"

"*Si* Rita. *Buenos noches*. Have you heard from my son recently?"

Strained silence filled the line. "No."

Juarez cleared his throat. "I…well, I haven't seen him tonight and—"

"I am sorry to say Bene told me to tell you not to call him right now. I tried to change his mind, but—"

Juarez Senior sipped his tequila, swirled the ice around in the glass. "I see."

"I told him this is not your fault *senor,* but right now he needs space. I will pray for you tonight on my Rosary."

Juarez clenched his teeth. "*Si. Gracias*, Rita. *Hasta Manana.*"

"*Buenos noches, senor.* I will see you in the morning and I will pray you two will be father and son again by then. I know Bene loves you and needs you right now."

"*Adios.*" Juarez hung up the phone, poured another tequila, shot it down. He pressed his eyes together and hoped this mess would be cleared up by morning.

Eighteen

Heavy traffic lined the two lane highway on the way out of Mexico City. Ricardo stared out the window while his 1970 Buick rattled down the interstate.

"Hey." The kid glanced at Ricardo. "I said hey."

Ricardo wanted to punch his nose for kicking his feet up on his dash. "Yeah?"

"Can you believe we got him?"

"Shut up and get your feet off of there, will you?" He slapped his legs.

"Yeah, but I'm just saying, this is big."

"*Stupido.* You are not supposed to say a word to anyone right now, not even to me."

They drove several miles farther when the kid spoke again. "Hey."

Up ahead a long line of traffic slowed to a stop. Damn. They needed to hurry. "What?"

"I've gotta take a leak."

Ricardo groaned. "You're kidding me, right?"

"No man, seriously."

Ricardo couldn't believe the boss allowed the kid to accompany him on such an important mission, especially when he already handled things himself. The kid was weak. "You know we're not supposed to stop until we get there. Boss' orders."

"Si, but I need to go bad, man." He pointed to the line of cars. "Besides, we're not going anywhere."

Ricardo sighed. "Aye Chihuahua, alright."

He pulled out of traffic and off on a side road near an agave cactus field.

"Here?" The kid scowled. "How am I gonna hide?"

Should I punch him out and throw him in the trunk now, or later? "Hide? You're gonna get out and piss, dumbass."

The kid didn't look happy and the traffic was awfully close to the car. He definitely didn't want to arouse any suspicions or have a police car pull over to see what they were doing. "Fine. I'll keep going." He continued down the gravel road about a half a mile and parked. "This better?"

The kid already opened the door with one leg outside. "Yep."

"Hurry or I'll leave you out here." Ricardo climbed out, stretched his legs, quickly changed out of his suit into cutoffs and a t-shirt, lit a cigarette and leaned against the car door.

Inside the trunk, the sound of loud knocking interrupted an otherwise quiet afternoon.

The kid finished relieving himself, walked up to the car and stared at the trunk. "Hey, you think we should see if he's okay?"

Ricardo blew smoke in his face. "No."

The kicking got louder.

"You sure, man? We have to bring him alive, right?"

Ricardo should've knocked Benito unconscious and they wouldn't be having this discussion right now. Better yet, he should be alone. "I don't know how you got this job. You don't have any of these, do you?" He lifted his chin and showed off a half dozen tattooed rings around his neck.

"No, but..."

"Or this?" He lifted his t-shirt, pulled it over his head and turned around. A giant blue feathered serpent covered most of his back, the tail feathers formed a line extending down his left leg past his knee, feather tips peeked out from his cutoffs.

"Hey that's cool, man, how long you had it?"

"Longer than you've been alive." He rubbed the end of the cigarette on the trunk lid. "Come on."

"I got these." The kid pulled his shirt collar back, revealing an extra thin scab around his neck, then turned his arm over and showed off a small jaguar tattoo. "So far anyway..."

"Oh, that's the problem," Ricardo laughed.

"What?"

"You're one of *them*."

"What do you mean?"

"Jaguar. I am Eagle. Everyone knows we're higher up on the ladder than you."

The kid kicked the ground. "Shut up."

Ricardo dropped his cigarette, stomped it into the dirt. "Who you telling to shut up?" He puffed up his chest and loomed over the kid with a menacing expression.

"Uh nobody man, just kidding."

Ricardo chuckled. "Get in the car."

The kicking noise got louder. Both men stared at the trunk.

Pain in the ass. He wished the damned man would stop struggling against his fate. "So you wanna take a peek, huh?"

The kid shrugged. "I'm only saying, he needs to be in good shape, right?"

"What the hell." Ricardo unlocked the trunk. "There you go."

Benito Juarez lay on his side, hands bound behind his back, legs tied with rope. A black hood covered his face.

Ricardo lit another cigarette. "Go ahead, check him if you want. I'm not touching him. It's against orders. If boss finds out we touched the Sacred One, I don't want to think about what he'd do to us. I'll tell him it was all you, jaguar boy."

The kid ignored Ricardo, reached into the trunk and ripped the hood off.

The young bearded man glared at them with hatred in his eyes. He immediately stopped mumbling through the tight cloth gag in his mouth. Caked blood ran down his forehead from a head wound and dried in his beard. He lay still and watched, first looking at the kid, then at Ricardo. His eyes registered disbelief.

The kid pointed to the restraint in Benito's mouth. "Should I untie this? It looks like it's hurting him."

Ricardo laughed. "What are you talking about? He's gonna be dead in a few days anyhow."

"Yeah, but…"

"But nothing."

"He is the risen god, isn't he?"

Ricardo sighed. "You really are a lightweight kid. If you're going to be anything in this organization, you have to learn to be tough. The gods command it. That means no compassion for the sacrifices, *comprende*?"

The kid stood firm with a doe eyed look on his face.

Ricardo sighed. "Aw alright. I guess if you want to do it, fine. But again, if boss man finds out, I won't hesitate to tell him who's bright idea it was, *comprende*?"

Without hesitation, the kid carefully removed the cloth, jerking his fingers out of the way in case the god tried to bite him.

Benito remained silent.

The kid proceeded to taunt his prey. "Hey. What's wrong with you? Speak up. Say something. Don't you want to run, huh? Wanna be free?"

Benito blinked, but said nothing.

Ricardo laughed. "You know, for a *Presidente*, you sure are *stupido*. Close the trunk, kid. We gotta get moving."

Nineteen

icardo. Bene couldn't believe his lifelong friend was responsible for all this misery. Did he kill Angela too?

He vaguely recalled the lifeless bodies of Jorge and Diego lying in a pool of blood outside the church. God! His blood ran cold thinking about it.

He turned his aching head slightly to the right and stared at the other young man who held him captive. Barely out of puberty and exceptionally tall and thin, this child must be brainwashed by some evil force. He didn't look capable of doing any of this on his own.

During his time in office, Bene desperately wanted to clean up the streets and give kids like this a chance. Now he realized he might not live long enough to achieve any of his lofty political visions.

He glanced back at Ricardo. What would compel Ricardo to do such a thing? Money? Power? Drugs? All three? No. All were powerful temptations for crime in modern Mexico, but this situation couldn't be about these alone. Something different motivated them, but what? And who did Ricardo work for?

If Ricardo came to him in trouble, Bene would have done anything to keep him from committing these murders.

He felt tempted to talk some sense into Ricardo, remind him how much money he could give them both if they set him free out here in the middle of nowhere. The highway couldn't be too far from here. He could walk back to the city. Maybe somebody would eventually drive by and give him a ride.

As for the kid, Bene would vow never to tell anyone about either of them. They could keep driving, start a new life elsewhere. He knew a great evil motivated Ricardo and he might not get through to him. The kid might be a different story. Maybe he hadn't been completely corrupted yet.

Benito still didn't say a word. He hated the idea of begging for his life but he would do anything to stop this homicidal maniac from butchering more innocent people.

"Aren't you gonna say something?" the kid asked.

Bene blinked.

"Huh?" He shoved him. "Aren't you gonna say somethin'?" He slapped Bene hard across the face.

He tasted his own blood, but kept quiet.

Ricardo laughed at his accomplice. "I didn't think you had it in you, kid."

The kid stood up straight, crossed his arms across his chest in a feeble attempt to puff himself up to a bigger size. "I am tough."

Ricardo put his cigarette out on the dirt. "Then shut the trunk and let's get going."

The boy slammed the trunk lid.

Bene wondered if he should've said something. No. He wouldn't give terrorists the satisfaction, even if it meant his early death. He stared into the dark and listened to the car start up and rattle down the road to nowhere.

***

That night Mario slept on the old lumpy sofa in his mother's living room. Springs stuck out and pushed into his back and his neck hurt from a bad pillow, but he didn't care. He would not sleep tonight no matter what.

He listened in the dark to the loud sobbing of his mother until sleep finally claimed her. At least her sorrow would go away until morning when the pain of her loss would be worse than today.

Tomorrow he would track down the people who did this to Angela and help his mom plan the funeral for later in the week. He might tell her about Angela's body, but only if she asked.

Just then, Bene crossed his mind and for some reason, a cold chill ran through him. Mario had a bad feeling this wasn't over yet. He felt it in his bones.

***

Outside the Martinez home, a man sat behind the wheel of a dark blue El Dorado and watched. Once the lights went out, he put his binoculars down, closed his eyes, and took a nap.

DAY TWO

Twenty

Sister Lucia Hernandez always arrived first at Cathedral Metropolitano every morning to open all the doors, wipe down the pews, prepare the offering plates and make the church beautiful for everyone who visited.

During her routine rounds, she walked to the door on the far back side of the church and tried to open it, but for some reason, today it wouldn't budge. She pushed with all her might, leaned her back against it until finally it cracked open, but only slightly.

She peeked into the side alleyway, wondering what in the world…and then she saw it. Fingers. She screamed. "Father Salazar, help! Come right away."

***

Father Salazar sat in his office in the back of the church when he heard Sister Hernandez screaming from inside the rectory. He tossed his Bible aside and ran into the Cathedral. "What is it, sister? What's wrong?"

The frantic nun cried and wrung her hands together. "Father. Please hurry. Someone is on the side of the building, and I'm afraid they're hurt."

He followed the sister outside, stunned to discover two men lying face first in an enormous pool of blood. Salazar flipped them over and gasped, making the sign of the cross over his heart. "Dear God, Sister. They're not hurt, they're dead."

The elderly nun screamed and cried, repeatedly crossing her heart. "What will we do?"

"Come inside." Salazar pulled the nun by the arm and whispered. "Shhh sister. Careful. Someone might still be out here." Father glanced both ways down the alley, then stepped back into the church, locked the door and pressed his back against it.

The nun continued to sob quietly, wringing her hands. "Dear Jesus, please help us."

Salazar was in shock. He wished he could erase the image from his mind of the two young men he'd known since childhood who were bloodied and dead in that alley. What was this world coming to?

Despite his faith, a great fear rose up in him. There was a reason why his faithful friend Benito hadn't shown up for Mass last night, and the priest had a good idea who was responsible. "Sister. We must call the *Palacio* immediately. *El Presidente* is in grave danger."

Twenty One

The following morning, Rita arrived to work earlier than normal. She couldn't sleep for all the events of yesterday. She told herself no matter what happened today, she would try her best to remain calm, hoping father and son could forgive and move on.

She went about her normal early morning duties of preparing the coffee, setting the conference room table for the daily staff breakfast, putting out the pastries and juices and making sure the fruit appeared fresh and any wilted grapes or dark bananas were tossed away. She hoped today would be better than yesterday.

"Ahem…"

Rita turned toward the voice. "Good morning, *Senor* Juarez. How are you today?"

Juarez Senior stood in the doorway. "I haven't heard from Bene. I stopped by his house to pick him up this morning, but he didn't answer the door or his phone. Did he call you?"

Rita dropped her spoon. The two always rode to work together. "What? You didn't see him today?"

Juarez looked worried. "No."

Terror clenched her heart. This couldn't be happening. Benito was always a conscientious young man. She couldn't believe he would hold such a grudge against his father. "You didn't ride in together?"

"No. Did The Boys pick him up?"

Rita shrugged. "They met him at the Cathedral yesterday afternoon, so yes, I assume so, *senor*."

Juarez got a faraway look in his eye. "Strange..."

"*Si*." Rita tried not to allow her fears to overtake her. Normally Bene's father rode in to the city center with his son and bodyguards every morning. They would never think of leaving him behind. Something was definitely wrong, even though she didn't want to believe it. "Do you think he's okay?"

"You tell me, Rita. You sent him to Mass last night, correct?"

"*Si*." Rita stomach tied in a knot. "But…"

Juarez stepped closer. "What?"

"Father Salazar called here late yesterday, *senor*, right before I left to go home. Something strange happened at the cathedral yesterday, a misunderstanding."

"Oh?"

"*Si*. I didn't think anything of it, but now that you mention it, I wonder… He said a new priest gave Bene Confession yesterday."

"What?"

"*Si*. Father Salazar ran into the other priest when he went out to find Bene for Mass, but he said Benito never showed up."

"Why didn't you tell me this sooner?" Juarez shouted.

"I don't know, *senor*. Father Salazar searched for Bene outside the confessional and in the sanctuary, but he'd already left with the guards. I didn't think anything of it."

"Have you seen the body guards yet today? Any of them?"

Rita realized her stupidity could prove fatal to Benito. "No."

Juarez squeezed his temples. "Oh my God, Rita."

At that moment, the phone rang, the red light flashed. *Emergency.* Only a handful of people had this restricted access number, and when it rang, it never meant good news. Yesterday morning it rang when Angela's body was discovered.

Rita froze.

Juarez glanced at her, his fears reflected in her eyes. "Let me answer this." He grabbed the phone. "*Hola*?" He listened. A great stillness settled over him. Quietly he hung up, sunk into the closest chair.

Rita's hands trembled. "*Senor*. What is it?"

Juarez swallowed hard. "I'm afraid our worst fears are upon us. Our Benito is missing."

"No. There must be a mistake." Rita couldn't believe her ears. This was all her fault. She should have made Bene stay in the office yesterday to be safe. "Who was that?"

"Father Salazar. He is coming over here right now to see us. It seems…" Juarez squeezed his fists tight and fought back tears.

Rita clutched her hands to her mouth. "What?"

"Salazar found Jorge and Diego dead in the alley next to the church this morning. Salazar said Bene didn't keep their Mass appointment yesterday like you said..." Juarez Senior gulped and walked to the window, staring down at the street. "This is a father's worst nightmare, Rita."

Rita's legs buckled beneath her, she fell back in her chair and wept. She knew something was wrong. She should have done something yesterday right when Father called her. Now it may be too late. "This is my fault."

No," Juarez said quietly. "It's not."

Twenty Two

The following morning, Mario showed up early to *Templo Mayor*. He didn't get a chance to go home, so his uniform looked slightly crinkled from the day before.

Lupe nearly spit her donut out when she saw him. "Mario? What are you doing here? They told me you took the day off."

"I know, but what am I supposed to do? I want to work. Besides, I need the money for funeral expenses and all."

"Mmm, *si*." She mumbled and buzzed him in.

Mario started to make his rounds and step on the dreaded wooden footbridge when Amelia Sanchez stopped him. "Shouldn't you be at home?"

"Uh, well…"

"Go home, Mario. I found someone to cover your shift today and even tomorrow if you need it."

Mario couldn't tell his boss he was an undercover spy for the *Presidente*. "*Muchos gracias*, *Senora* Sanchez. I don't know what else to do, but work. Please. Let me stay. It keeps my mind off things."

"Are you sure?" Her kind eyes seemed sincerely concerned. "This must be so traumatic for you."

"*Si Senora.*"

"And your mother? How is she taking this?"

Mario's eyes fell to the floor. "Not so well."

"Then go take care of her."

Agh! Mario hated this. Apparently his pleas to stay weren't working so he tried something else. "I need to work. My family needs the money for funeral expenses."

Sanchez shook her head. "No Mario. We will pay for all expenses. We will even pay for you to speak to someone. A counselor."

"*Muchos gracias*, but please, I must work so my life can go on."

Senora Sanchez hesitated for a moment. "Okay, but tell me if you need time off to make arrangements, *comprende*?"

"*Si, gracias.*" Relieved, Mario started down the footbridge. He didn't need counseling, he needed to find Angela's killers.

Sanchez called after him. "You don't have to work out here today. Come inside and guard the doors."

Mario didn't want to work inside. He needed to study the scene and observe the investigators and hopefully overhear something important. He didn't want to arouse any suspicions though, so he followed Sanchez out the gate to the Museo entrance and noticed men down below still working in the Eagle Chamber. "Why are they still here?"

"They're still investigating," Sanchez explained.

Mario was confused. Why would they have investigators poking around with tourists on site? "But we're open today, right?"

"*Si*, the visitors won't be allowed to go inside the chambers themselves anyway. The officers want to continue analyzing soil samples and see if anything turns up."

The front façade of the Museo appeared reminiscent of an old Spanish styled house with six windows stacked in two rows of three. "*Aqui.*" Sanchez held the door for him.

"*Gracias.*" Mario felt the cold blast of air hit him the moment he walked inside the Museo. This could be his chance to find out more about the staff and see if any of them were involved in the murder. He also needed time to learn more about the organizational structure of the *museo* and find out about the restricted area downstairs. Plus there was one more topic Mario needed to get clear about. "I met with Director Montoya yesterday."

"*Si,* he mentioned it."

"I'm confused, *Senora*. I thought you were Director."

"I am Curator, *Senor* Montoya is Director for our Board."

"Oh." Maybe Montoya's rudeness was just that, nothing more.

Sanchez stopped at the top of the stairs. "You can make rounds in here. The doors will open to the public in ten minutes, like always. Keep an eye on everyone inside, make sure they don't disrupt any of our exhibitions or handle any of the artifacts. Watch the handbags and purses. Report anything out of the ordinary directly to me. Also, security cameras are set up in each of the eight *salas*, or floors."

"Does someone monitor them?"

"Normally staff reviews the tape and watches people, but lately we are a bit short on help, so the answer to the question is no, but it's all on video."

"Do you film outside too?"

"We used to and I wish we still did. If you're asking about the Eagle Chamber, unfortunately the construction crew removed the cameras from the area last week."

"Last week?" *How convenient*... He wondered how the security camera photos of Angela were taken. He needed to interview those workers, see what company they worked for. Not now though. He wasn't sure whether or not Sanchez was on his side.

Sanchez sighed. "I'm sorry, Mario. I promise we will do all we can to find your sister's killers."

"*Muchos gracias, Senora* Sanchez." He practically bit his tongue to keep from asking her about those construction crew members. For now, he kept these thoughts to himself. One other situation still haunted him.

Once Sanchez turned the corner safely out of sight, Mario headed straight downstairs where he left Rosa yesterday. He couldn't shake the feeling something bad happened to her.

The only light in the basement came from three floor to ceiling glass windows in a corner. Mario walked around, shone his flashlight and finally found the light switch panel on the far wall and clicked it on.

He walked up to the exact place where Rosa sat yesterday and realized he'd been right all along. A few red droplets dried onto the stone seat. He walked toward the door to the restricted area and shined his light on the tile and found red spots there too. Could this be residue from her mop, or had Rosa succumb to a similar ill fate as his sister? He tried the lock on the doors again, but they still wouldn't open. Mario pulled the radio from his belt and called up to the office. "*Senor*a Sanchez?"

Her voice crackled over the speaker. "*Si*."

"Did you see Rosa today?"

She hesitated. "No. Is she not downstairs yet?"

"No, *Senor*a. Is she on the schedule today?"

"*Si,* she should have clocked in already."

Mario didn't want to get anyone in trouble if he was mistaken. "I'm sure she is here somewhere. I will look again for her and let you know."

He needed to tell Bene about this, discreetly, of course. He pulled out his cell and turned it on. It took a moment for the signal to register from the basement of the *Museo*, but within a few seconds, it amped up and he dialed.

Bene's phone rang and rang. A generic message came on. The recorder was full, so Mario couldn't leave a message. *Damn.* He dialed the number again, slower this time, in case his missed a digit. This time, the phone rang incessantly without any answer. *Bene. Answer the phone. I need to reach you.* Finally the same recording came on. He didn't have the number to Bene's office, so for now, this discussion would have to wait.

He scanned the basement ceiling and spotted two small metal cameras in the corners. One pointed directly at the staircase and the large glass display filled with ancient Aztec masks, the other pointed at the restricted area. He stood on the built in tile seat where Rosa sat yesterday, and pulled the camera from its stand. He knew he shouldn't do this, but if something happened to Rosa, it would surely be recorded on this tape. If not, he could replace it in an hour or two after he took a look. Since Sanchez said they were short staffed lately, Mario figured nobody would notice.

He turned the camera over, studied each side trying to open it. Finally he saw a small button on the back, pressed it and it popped open. He slipped the tape into his left sock for safekeeping, closed the unit and started to put it back.

"Ahem." A voice interrupted from behind him. "What do you think you're doing, Martinez?"

Mario jumped and nearly fell off the bench. He spun around and saw Montoya standing at the foot of the stairs, giving him the evil eye.

Twenty Three

By the time Salazar arrived to the Palacio, the *policia* were busy interviewing a frantic Juarez Senior who ran to the door when he saw his old friend. "Salazar, thank God you're here. What happened?" He put an arm around the priest and led him to a chair around the conference table.

The Priest clasped his hands in prayer and sighed. "I'm afraid Benito's lifelong friends Jorge and Diego are dead. I found them in the alley outside the church this morning.

"Dear God in heaven!" Rita said.

Juarez' mouth fell open. "How?"

Salazar cleared his throat. "I've not seen anything quite like this. They were gutted, their hearts torn from their chest cavities…" His lower lip began to quiver.

Rita burst into tears, covered her mouth. "What does this mean for poor Bene?"

The policia officer took diligent notes. "Anything else, Father Salazar?"

"*Si.* I planned to see Benito at Mass and Sister Hernandez mentioned a new priest would replace me in the confessional. I normally never allow such breaches in protocol, but since I assumed Benito requested it, I made an exception. God have mercy on my soul, I should never have allowed it."

Juarez Senior patted him on the back. "This is not your fault, Father."

"So you're saying you did not conduct the *Presidente's* confession yesterday?" the officer asked.

"No." Salazar lowered his eyes to hide his shame.

The officer put his notepad down, stared the priest in the eye. "If you didn't, who did?"

"A man named Martinez. He called himself *Father* Martinez, but I can tell you with great certainty, this man was no priest."

Juarez leapt from his chair. "Did you say *Martinez*?"

The priest nodded. "*Si, senor.* Father Martinez."

Juarez pounded his fist. "Father Salazar is correct. This was no priest. I want a warrant issued for Mario Martinez' on charges of murder, kidnapping and treason."

***

Bene listened for the fortieth or fiftieth time to the far distant sound of his cell phone ringing. His eyes pressed closed with such exhaustion, he could not wake up to save his life.

Someone reached in his breast pocket and removed it. "You don't need this anymore, but we do."

The familiar sound of his former friend Ricardo echoed in his ears.

***

Ricardo held Bene's phone in his hand while it rang again. He glanced at the caller ID. *Mario Martinez.* He laughed and slipped the cell phone into his pocket for safekeeping.

Twenty Four

Mario slipped the security tape from the Museo camera into his sock when someone interrupted. He turned around.

Montoya squinted at him through his thick eyeglasses. "What are you doing?"

Slowly releasing his grip on the camera, Mario set it neatly in its stand. "*Senor* Montoya. I wanted to make sure this fixture is secure and hoped to find video footage to help solve my sister's murder." *And Rosa's disappearance which no one around here seems to acknowledge.*

Montoya scowled. "What business is it of yours? The policia are handling this and you were told to go home yesterday."

Mario decided to ignore Montoya and continue to act helpful. He wasn't going home. "I also checked the door to the restricted area, to make sure it is still locked tight."

Montoya glared at him and pointed to the door. "That area is off limits. *Comprende?*"

Mario climbed down from the bench. "*Si senor*, which is why—"

Before he could finish his thought, over a dozen armed policia with guns drawn rushed down the stairs interrupting the conversation with the thunderous sound of their boots slamming the concrete floor. All pointed their weapons in Mario's direction and encircled him so he couldn't get away. "Mario Martinez?"

He threw up both hands. "*Si?*"

"Mario Martinez, you are under arrest for high treason, murder and kidnapping. Step aside, *senor*." The policia pushed Montoya to the side and forcefully grabbed hold of Mario, cuffing him, slapping him to the ground, blackening his right eye and bloodying his lip before frisking his pant pockets and uniform jacket.

He wiped blood off on his sleeve. "Wait. You've made a terrible mistake."

The policia slapped him again and pulled him to his feet. "Shut up and come with us."

Twenty Five

The Mexican People's Party or *Partido del La Gente* was created in 1980 The fledgling group originally considered a non-entity by the other three major political parties, consisted of radical left-winged elitist Christian Fundamentalists who claimed to be more aligned with the true lifestyle of Christ and his disciples than any other group. These socialists believed the government and the wealthy exploited the poor for their own means and society should return to a state of social and economic equality for all people, similar to the times of Christ.

The current leader Pepe Ayala insisted on recruiting strong players to expand his vision throughout Mexico. He kept up with current events and read every single newspaper cover to cover daily. He quickly recognized the talent of a young newspaper columnist, Angela Martinez, who wrote passionate weekly editorials about the poorest of the poor and her belief that equality should prevail for all citizens. Ayala began courting the young journalist first by sending complimentary letters about her work, then gifts, which increased in value as the months went on, until finally, after a brief private meeting, Ayala convinced her to work for him.

Ayala realized he could not keep the news of Angela's death to himself for long. Word would eventually leak to staff members, so the political leader held a closed door conference first thing the following morning after receiving a set of photos yesterday. After explaining the situation, Ayala stared at each of the dozen gathered before him. "So, who is responsible for this?" He slapped the photos in the center of the conference room table for all to see. "Tell me!"

The blank-faces staffers seemed stunned, while others burst out into tears at the sight of the horrific photos.

"I want answers." Ayala pounded his fist on the desk and a small sculpture went crashing to the floor in tiny pieces. "Are our enemies starting to get intimidated by us?"

The newest and most prized member of the elite PG staff, Angela spent long hours working alongside their leader in closed-door meetings and shared information that nobody but the two of them knew about.

The staff passed the photos around, whispering amongst themselves.

"I'm sure I don't have to tell you people, Angela's unusual and untimely death will bring the media and the government into our space and put this operation under a microscope. We all know this is the last thing we need right now. So tell me." Ayala pounded the conference table again. "Who did this? Huh? Tell me!"

Angela's diligent work as spin-doctor successfully led the media away from her boss and the implications that he coerced illegal monies from big business with environmental political agendas.

Some political leaders, including those from the Presidente's own party, demanded Ayala turn himself in immediately and go to prison.

Ayala did his best to cover any paper trails and when Angela questioned him directly about the accusations against him, he consistently told her they fabricated lies to oust him from office.

Although most public scrutiny of Ayala's politics came from the Presidente's political party, Ayala feared many who turned on him were members of the PRD or *Partido of Democratic Revolution.*

In the past several elections the two parties joined forces in order to control a greater majority of the votes. *Partido La Gente* wasn't successful in elections as of yet, but they slowly gained grass roots support and growing steadily in numbers. They hoped before Juarez' second term the party would include enough members and political clout to actually give the incumbent a serious run for his money.

The leader of the PRD was friendly to Ayala's face, but secretly harbored resentment toward the charismatic leader and some closest to Ayala feared he wanted him out of the way so he could control both organizations.

Nobody answered him so Ayala continued his rampage. "Is the PRD sending a message to us? If so, they better be prepared to receive our answer."

The staff cheered and clapped.

Vicious rumors about *Partido La Gente* emerged out of nowhere and the media ate it up. The staff assumed PRD was responsible, although nobody could prove it. The height of the trouble happened to come right before Angela came on board. Ayala remembered Angela's continuous warnings about PRD, but he never heeded any of them. Angela held a clear and mature grasp of politics and the situation Ayala faced in the coming months if he expected to maintain his power and continue to gain political ground.

"Well?" Ayala shouted. "Will any of you say anything? Do any of you know who is messing with us and why?"

Nobody said a word.

"What good are any of you? Angela Martinez was my only team member who bothered to dig deep to help our cause and now she's gone." Ayala paced around the table, staring every staffer in the eye. He picked up one of the grizzly photos and held it high for everyone to see. "I fear we are vulnerable to someone, *amigos*. The question is, *to who?*"

Twenty Six

Ricardo hadn't slept a wink between dealing with the kid and corralling and the would-be-god into his new quarters.

With Bene sufficiently drugged with the prescribed mixture of hallucinogenic *pulque*, Ricardo anxiously awaited his meeting with the group leader when he would offer up the spoils of last night's victory. He tucked Bene's phone in his pocket and turned to the kid. "Hey."

He leaned against the wall napping and jumped when Ricardo startled him from sleep. "Uh yeah?"

"Where's the box?"

The kid rubbed his eyes, scrambling around searching for his knapsack. "Give me a second."

"Hurry up. We don't have all day."

He reached deep into the sack and pulled it out. "Here you go."

Ricardo snapped it from his hands. "Good."

The kid stood up, straightened his shirt. "Hey wait. I wanna come."

"You need to stay here, guard the god." Benito still appeared unconscious, but you could never be too careful with a situation this important. Somebody needed to keep watch on him twenty four seven.

"But he can't go anywhere."

Ricardo growled. This kid could be such a pain in his ass. "Alright, come on, but keep your mouth shut while I speak, you got it?"

He nodded.

They opened the door to the one room hacienda, locking it up behind them, and stepped out into the morning sun. A half mile walk over the desert floor took them to the base of the pyramid where several other Eagle Warriors in full regalia stood watch outside.

Each warrior wore a thick peacock feathered headdress. Bodies covered with intricate designs, they all sported several black rings around their necks.

The kid tapped Ricardo's shoulder. "Hey. What is the name of this place again?"

Ricardo shoved his hands away. "If you don't know by now, you don't deserve to know."

One of the guards approached with a long obsidian spear in his hand. "Who goes there?"

Ricardo wasn't at all intimidated by these men, not any of them. He more than earned his keep. "We are here to bring spoils to the Hummingbird on the Left." Ricardo carefully followed protocol by using the code name for the feathered man who embodied the god *Huitzilopochtli*.

The guard grunted and led them around to the south side of the pyramid to an open door, also flanked with sentinels. Inside, the feathered one sat atop an altar covered in fresh fruit, cacao beans, vanilla, chili powder and sliced prickly pear cacti, amongst other things. He sipped on a beverage, careful not to smudge the thick blue paint covering his face and mouth.

The guard announced them. "*Senor*, your servants bring spoils for the altar."

The feathered man smiled. "Leave us. Both of you, step forward."

Ricardo resented the kid being here at such an important moment in his life. "*Senor*," he bowed. "We bring offerings from our journey to capture *Quetzalcoatl*." Ricardo reached out and handed over the stone box. He watched the leader intently. Ricardo only saw him from a distance before today. He felt honored and humbled in the Great One's presence.

"*Muy bueno*." The leader smiled and lifted the lid revealing the lifeless heart. "*Bueno.* Who does this belong to?"

Ricardo proudly lifted his chest. "I told you, *senor*, this is one of the two presidential guards I sacrificed yesterday in accordance with your methods."

The leader twisted the box in his hands and smiled. "*Bueno.* And the other? Where is it?" He glanced over Ricardo's shoulder toward the kid.

"The other guard is also sacrificed, Great One, however we left the heart behind."

The leader's eyes grew wide and he spoke with calm intensity. "I see…"

Ricardo sensed the leader's displeasure, so he scrambled for excuses. "*Senor*, he is finished, I promise. We had very little time to—"

He held up a hand to silence him. "Enough. He is dead, correct?"

Ricardo nodded. "*Si*."

"And you secured our god and began preparations for ceremony?"

"*Si*."

"Where is he?"

"In the house you reserved for him, My Lord."

He clapped his hands. "Ah, *magnifico*. You've done well, Eagle Warrior."

Ricardo's pride swelled. "*Gracias, Senor.*"

The Great One stretched his arms wide. "Now come forward so I may present you with your reward."

Without hesitation, Ricardo stepped closer, grinning from ear to ear. He dreamed of this day for so many years. His time had come at last.

The Great One rest his hands on Ricardo's shoulders. "Close your eyes, brave warrior."

Ricardo followed orders. He waited a split second before hearing the sound of his cracking breastbone. Shocked by the stabbing pain of the obsidian blade piercing his chest cavity, Ricardo opened his eyes. From this vantage point, he got a good look at the pale green eyes, the high cheekbones of the painted face. He noticed how the excess makeup collected in the heavy lines and wrinkles around his mouth and eyes. He gazed at his executioner and croaked. "Why?"

The feathered man laughed. "Next time, bring both hearts. Meanwhile, your services here are no longer needed." He clutched the end of the blade and hoisted it higher in his gut.

The kid gasped and backed up against the wall.

Twenty Seven

Juarez paced around the office while Salazar and Rita prayed. Soon, the policia stormed down the long corridors of the *Palacio* leading a prisoner by the arms. "Bring him in here."

The officers threw Mario on the floor and kicked him. "Here he is, *Senor* Juarez."

"Stop." Juarez demanded. "Do not hurt him. Keep the cuffs on him and all of you wait outside. Close the door."

Most of the officers left immediately, while two lingered.

"Out," Juarez directed. "That goes for you too."

"But *senor*, he is a dangerous criminal," one of the remaining officers said.

Juarez pointed to the door. "I don't care. We have important things to discuss. Leave us now, close the door tight and wait outside. I will call when we need you."

"*Si, Senor* Juarez." They immediately turned to go.

Juarez stared at the brother of his son's trouble-making dead girlfriend and wondered what would possess Martinez to murder Bene's guards. He must be temporarily insane and went into a fit of rage, blaming Benito for his sister's demise. There could be no other explanation. "Get up."

Martinez did not budge.

Juarez kicked Mario slightly with the side of his dress shoe. "I said get off the floor, Martinez. Now."

Mario slowly rolled to one side and leaned himself up on his elbows while staggering to his feet with cuffed hands. "*Senor* Juarez, I—"

"Enough." Juarez turned to the priest. "Father Salazar, is this the man you saw with Bene yesterday?"

Salazar clasped his hands in prayer and nodded. "*Si.*"

"But I can explain, *Senor*," Martinez said.

Juarez slapped him across the face, sending him to the ground again. "What do you mean killing my son's guards and what did you do with Benito? Tell me now, and your life *might* be spared."

Rita burst into tears and ran to the corner of the room, covering her eyes.

Juarez glanced at Rita and found her behavior utterly annoying. She'd always been overly emotional during the twenty plus years he'd known her. He turned back to Mario. "What do you say for yourself, Martinez?"

Mario rolled over again and pressed himself up. "I did not do anything to *El Presidente*, *Senor*. I met him in the Cathedral, yes, so we could talk in private, make a plan."

Juarez tried to read Martinez, see if he was telling the truth or not. "What kind of *plan*?"

***

Several of Mario's ribs felt broken, and he could hardly lift himself up off the floor to continue his story. Confused, he didn't know what to say or not say without violating his trust with Bene. Just because he was in pain and potentially a ton of trouble, Mario made a vow to Benito and he refused to break it. "I told you, I met him at Mass so we could discuss Angela's murder. That was all. I told him what I know, but so far, we haven't learned much—"

Juarez crossed his arms in front of his chest, pressed his nose near Mario's. "And you expect me to believe that?" He turned to Rita. "You hear that, Rita? My son is missing, his friends are dead and Martinez here expects me to buy his stupid story."

Mario's blood ran cold. He knew nothing about any friends, his only concern was Benito. "What happened, *Senor* Juarez? Did something happen to Bene? I tried calling him earlier, but he didn't answer."

"That is none of your business until you tell me what kind of plans the two of you made yesterday and why you impersonated a priest."

Mario needed to stay out of prison, but he also needed to maintain his composure, not give away too much. "I don't know if you knew my sister, Angela Martinez?"

Juarez scowled. "Of course I knew her."

"Benito called me here yesterday..."

Rita stepped forward. "This is true. I saw *Senor* Martinez with Bene this time yesterday morning."

Juarez turned to Rita and scowled before glancing at Mario again. "And?"

"Benito seemed very upset, *senor*. He asked me to go back to work and see if I could find out anything else about her death. He told me to meet him in the confessional yesterday afternoon to give him a report."

"That is preposterous. Why wouldn't he meet you there?"Juarez asked.

"*Yo no se.*" Mario didn't want to tell Juarez Senior his son didn't trust him. "*Senor Presidente* and I talked briefly yesterday afternoon before the body guards came to get him. That's when I left the confessional and ran into Father Salazar, right after Bene left with his personal guards."

"And did you see these men, Martinez?"

Mario scratched his head. "Well no, but I heard them knock on the confessional and lead him away."

Juarez turned to the priest. "Is this true, Salazar?"

Salazar sat on the sofa, his hands in prayer. "*Si,* I ran into Martinez by accident. He gave me a stupid story about meeting Benito at the Cathedral in Districto Federal, as if someone like him could ever set foot in the place. I knew then Martinez lied. I should have called the *policia* right then and there. If I had, Benito might still be with us."

Mario defended himself. "But *Senor*, Bene left to go to the Palacio with his bodyguards after we talked."

"His guards are dead."

Mario's heart sank. The reality finally hit him. "What?"

"*Si*. Both of them were found this morning outside the Cathedral, or didn't you already know about that, *Senor* Martinez?"

Mario's hands trembled. "No."

"Benito had an appointment with me right after his Confession, Martinez. Only he never showed up."

"But Bene never mentioned Mass to me, *Senor* Juarez, I swear." Mario thought back to the arrangements and his stomach churned. "Oh no. You mean—"

"Didn't you kill them all for vengeance for what happened to your sister?"

"No *Senor*. No. Besides, how could I when the Father saw me leave out the back door?"

Everyone shared a brief moment of silence as each considered the other's viewpoints.

"This is all my fault." Rita wailed. "I set up Mass and I should never have let him out of this office after what happened to Angela."

"Shut up." Juarez yelled and turned back to Mario. "So Martinez, you are saying you did not see Bene again?"

"No *Senor*."

"Then why did you meet him in secret and how did you slip inside the cathedral unnoticed?"

"Bene and I planned this when I came to see him yesterday. He told me to enter in the back right at

4:00p.m., change into robes and wait for him. *Senor*, your son told me he feared for his life. He did not want to tell these plans to anyone but me, because he wanted help to bring the killers to justice before they could get to him."

"Well they already have, Martinez. They killed his two of his best men in the process, and the third's gone missing."

Mario fell to his knees and put his head in his hands. "Oh no, *Senor*. I swear will do whatever I can to help you get him back. You have my word."

Twenty Eight

The kid, whose actual name was Carlos Ortiz, trembled like a leaf in the wind at the sight of his mentor Ricardo flayed open before his very eyes. The evil leader ripped Ricardo's still beating heart from his chest cavity and held it up in the dim light of the pyramid. "What's wrong, boy?"

Carlos didn't say a word. Nobody in the cult knew his real name and right now he was glad they didn't.

The Great One stared a hole in him. "What is wrong? Have you not participated in sacrifice before?"

He hid his shaking hands behind his back. "*Si.*"

He beckoned him with a finger. "Come closer."

Carlos stood still, his feet planted solid on the dirt floor. He prepared to fight if necessary to avoid the same fate as Ricardo.

"I said come closer…"

Carlos took a half step.

"Closer. Now."

Carlos realized his end was near unless he could run outside across the field, which was pointless to even think about. Any one of those Eagle Warriors outside could stomp him with the sole of his boot. For the first time since getting involved with this group, Carlos was officially in over his head. "*Si, senor*."

The leader calmed down, chuckled under his breath. "You have nothing to fear, my boy. Believe me. The gods reserved a place for you in the afterlife. I promise." The leader reached the long thin blade of his sword out so it nicked the boy's neck slightly. "Don't be afraid," he lowered the boy's shirt collar with the blade, just enough so he could see the fresh wounds of the tattoo on his neck. "I see... you got your markings already, did you?"

Carlos ran his index finger over the newly formed scab, hoping it might provide him safety now. "*Si*."

"Before you produced a heart?" The Great One ticked his tongue. "That's against the rules."

The boy backed away from the prickly tip of the blade still dripping with Ricardo's blood. "*Si*."

"What will you offer in exchange for this mark?"

Carlos gulped. "Uh, I don't know, *senor*."

"Is there another heart here you aren't telling me about?" He poked Carlos' chest with the tip of the blade, staining his shirt in red.

Carlos didn't know the correct answer to this question. Obviously his heart wasn't an option. He could lie and offer to go get one from the car and run, but the warriors would likely shoot him with poison tipped arrows in the back. Instead, he decided to be honest. "No."

The leader slowly studied him as a man might eye any meal before cutting into it. "Well then, you must leave something behind until you can bring me a heart. What will you offer the gods today?"

Carlos reached into his pocket, pulled out his last few pesos and handed them over. "*Aqui.*"

The leader laughed so hard, Carlos thought he might topple from his stony throne. "Oh my boy. You are so naïve. The gods *pesos* are made of gold. What makes you think they want these worthless things?" He knocked the money from the boy's hands, cutting his palm in the process.

"Pardon, *senor*," Carlos apologized. "It is all I have right now. I promise I will get you something else. I can go get it now and be back very soon."

"No. The gods demand something more now. You stand before them in this sacred place, do you not?"

Before he could step away, Carlos felt the knife cut him. "Ouch." He screamed as his right earlobe toppled to the floor.

"This will do." The leader stabbed it with the tip of his blade, brought it up to his hand, dusted the dirt off and removed it, placing it on the stone beside him. "For now…"

Carlos started to get up and felt another rush of pain shoot through his head as the leader blindsided him with another stroke of the blade. "Ah." He cried and fell back again.

The leader stabbed his other lobe, offering it to Carlos. "Here. You must take this."

Carlos held his hands to his bleeding head and whimpered.

The feathered man pushed it toward him with the knife tip. "Come on. Take it, unless you want to make the ultimate sacrifice right now."

Carlos reluctantly stepped forward and pulled his left earlobe off the blade.

"Now go on. Put it in your pocket and remember this. You owe the gods and if you don't produce, you will wind up like your friend, *comprende*?"

"Uh huh." Carlos tried not to cry. He stuffed his fleshy lobe into his left front pocket of his jeans and started toward the door.

The leader laughed. "Godspeed, young man. Go and fetch us what we most desire. *Andale.* Quick. Be back here tomorrow or the gods will make you pay."

The feathered man noticed the cell phone fall from the dead man's pocket. He reached down and grabbed it, smearing blue paint on the numbers, scrolled through the list to see the caller ID. Several unknown calls, and one from a name he recognized – *Mario Martinez.* He smiled and laughed to himself.

Twenty Nine

Juarez Senior stared at the young man lying on the floor. "This is an outrage. My son is missing and none of us have any idea where he is. How did we allow this to happen?"

"I swear, *Senor* Juarez, I am telling you the God's truth." Mario held his hands up in surrender.

Juarez could see by the look in Martinez' eyes he told the truth, but it still infuriated him that this mess endangered his son's life. "Fine, but that still doesn't excuse the fact that we each allowed the *Presidente* of Mexico to slip out from under us all, even you, Martinez. And now several hours passed, and none of you can tell me where my Bene is, or if he is even still alive."   The thought of this mess brought mixed feelings of rage and sorrow to the aging Juarez, who already buried Bene's mother years earlier. To lose his son would be completely unbearable. He turned to look at Salazar. "What do you think?"

The priest nervously rubbed the rosary beads around his neck. "He is telling the truth. I can feel it."

Juarez scowled. "Are you sure?"

Salazar nodded. "*Si.*"

"Why did he lie about being a priest then?"

Martinez stepped forward. "Because…"

"Enough." Juarez shouted. "I am talking to you, Salazar."

"He lied, yes, but…" Salazar shook his head. "I don't know. Bene must trust this young man. He loved his sister, you know."

Juarez threw his hands in the air. "Aye, aye, aye. I can't believe this. Will somebody please tell me what happened to Benito? Now, *por favor*."

***

Mario wanted to further defend himself, but decided against it. His face and ribs couldn't take much more abuse.

Juarez took a few steps back, his eyes filled with tears, his anger turned to sadness. "Why can't you tell me about my son?"

Praying the words coming out of his mouth would be enough to convince everyone of his innocence, Mario cleared his throat. "*Senor* Juarez, I swear on the Holy Bible I didn't hurt Benito. My sister loved with your son. Why would I want to dishonor her memory by doing something to him? *Senor*, we are on the same side here. I swear it." Mario hoped he said enough to persuade them to let him go. Perhaps he could share a bit more about the mission to foster trust between them. "Also, something strange happened yesterday I think you should know."

Juarez' eyebrows perked up. "Oh? What?"

Mario talked a mile a minute. "Well *senor*, Benito made it clear he wouldn't tell anyone about our plans for safety's sake, but when I showed up to the Cathedral yesterday, a huge man, one of *El Presidente's* guards waited for me when I arrived. He let me in and—"

"What did he look like?" Juarez interrupted.

"Huge man, round face, tattoo around his collar—"

Juarez glanced at Salazar. "Ricardo."

Salazar nodded. "*Si*."

Juarez stepped behind Benito's desk. Several pictures lined up in a row on the credenza. He grabbed the one in the middle, handed it to Martinez. "Him?"

Mario saw the two men who followed him yesterday with the third who met him at the Cathedral door. "*Si*."

Juarez turned to his old friend. "What do you make of this, Father?"

The priest shrugged. "I don't know. I didn't see Ricardo yesterday. Maybe the killers kidnapped Benito and Ricardo."

A heavy silence filled the room as they all silently pondered the other possibility – Benito and Ricardo were dead too. Mario couldn't believe this was happening. If he'd only known, he would have done anything to keep Bene from harm.

Juarez sighed. "If they did capture them both, it would be a mixed blessing. Any of them would fight to the death for Benito, especially Ricardo."

"Ricardo could save him, *senor.*" Salazar kept a hopeful tone. "Benito is a powerful man. Perhaps they will contact us and demand money."

"We can't give in to terrorists," Juarez said, "But I will do what I must to get Benito returned safe."

"Ricardo wasn't at work yesterday," Rita said.

Mario felt ill. What did that mean?

Juarez defended him. "I'm sure Ricardo had his reasons. That has nothing to do with this. Martinez saw Ricardo so he must have been back on the job by the afternoon."

Unless... Mario cringed. Perhaps there was a reason the man didn't show up to work. He thought about saying something, but kept quiet. Juarez Senior obviously wasn't ready to accept anything of that nature. Besides, Benito hadn't officially gone missing yet, there was no ransom note or demand made.

"*Senor.*" Rita interrupted, fluttered a paper around. "*Senor.*"

Juarez snapped. "What?"

Rita handed him the document. "I forgot about this. It's a note from Benito. Yesterday before he left to go to the Cathedral, he asked me to hire Mario Martinez as one of his private Presidential guards effective immediately." She lowered her eyes and wiped her tears. "He asked me not to tell you, *Senor* Juarez…he was so angry at you …"

"So you kept this from me?" Juarez waved the letter in her face and growled.

"No, no *senor*. I promise." She crossed her heart. "I just now remembered. Bene told me from his own mouth, Mario is his trusted friend. We must honor his wishes."

For the first time in an hour, Mario breathed a sigh of relief. "*Senor*, I hope you believe me now. My concern is not for myself, it is for Benito. I'm worried."

"And you think I'm not?"

Mario shrugged. "He has been missing quite some time now."

"Don't you think I know that?" Juarez shouted. "Thanks to all of you, he might even be dead."

Rita gasped and brought her hands to her mouth. "You don't mean that, *Senor*."

Mario needed to get things under control in a hurry. "*Attencion*. Listen. I know our feelings and emotions are running hot, but we all need to work together quickly to bring Benito home. If you will trust me, *Senor* Juarez, I swear I will do whatever I can to find him and bring these tyrants to justice. I will gladly give my life to see *El Presidente* safely returned to you, *Senor*."

Juarez calmed down. "But how? Who do you think is doing all this?"

Mario smiled for the first time all day. "I have a very good idea I know exactly who is involved and if you will release me, I will go there right now and find out."

Thirty

C arlos held his palms to his bloody ears and ran out of the pyramid. He pushed his way through the lines of Eagle Warriors, glad to see they did not follow. They laughed amongst themselves, some speaking freely in the dead language, while others audibly made fun of his cowardice. He didn't care. He needed to get out of this place and away from these people before he got himself killed.

He ran across the open space, back to the house where they held the god in preparation for ceremony. Luckily Ricardo left him in charge of the keys. He unlocked the door and took a look around the room, making sure he didn't leave anything behind.

The *Presidente* groaned in pain, tossed and turned. Thankfully he was still alive. Carlos finally realized these people were mentally sick. He needed to get back to Mexico City and get Benito some help.

He pulled his bloodied right hand away from his head, stained red thanks to the gash in his ear where his lobe used to be and the other cut in the center of his palm. He noticed a pile of plain white towels stacked neatly in the corner. He picked up several, tying off his right hand, taking the others and dabbing his head wounds. He hoped he would not bleed to death, he didn't think he would, but he couldn't be sure right now. All he knew is that he needed to get *El Presidente* out of here and get them both some help.

He searched the room for the special keys to unlock the thick metal cuffs on the Presidente's arms and legs, but after a few minutes, he couldn't find them. He remembered Ricardo took those.

Carlos went to the *Presidente's* bedside, fumbled with the restraints. "Don't worry. I will help you."

Just then, the door opened. "What are you doing?"

Carlos spun around. A young girl stared at him. "*Nada.* Making sure these are on tight."

She took a closer look at him and gasped when she saw all the blood. "What happened to you?"

He tried to brush it off. "*No problemo.*"

"Are you sure?" She walked over lifted one of the fresh white towels to his head. "You don't look alright."

Carlos wished he could take *El Presidente* with him, but with her here and who knows who else outside the door, he realized to do so would be a sure death sentence. He would go for help by himself and bring the authorities to find Benito later. He pressed the towel up to his ear, soaking it in crimson. "*Gracias.* I need to go now. You will watch him, *si*?"

She nodded.

He hoped so, she didn't look more than twelve. "Take care of him?"

"*Si.*"

"Good. I have to run." *If she only knew…* Carlos grabbed his bag and went outside to find the car.

Thirty One

After his unfruitful staff meeting, Ayala stomped back to his office, infuriated about the mess with Angela Martinez and the political firestorm sure to follow. Somebody wanted to put an end to all his organization had worked for all these years. But who?

He sifted through the crime scene photos again, unable to believe anyone capable of such a heinous crime. He didn't want his staff to know, but Ayala feared for his own life more than anything else. With such a bunch of imbeciles working for him and the only brains other than his own now buried, there was no telling what might become of him and the PT.

He dropped the photos and walked over to his window and watched people walk around the *Zocalo*. He wished he could shake those images from his mind.

Suddenly, his door was kicked in by the *policia*.

Ayala threw up his hands, backed up against the window. "Hey, what do you think you're—"

A half a dozen heavily armed policia pointed automatic weapons in his face. One stepped forward. "Pepe Ayala?"

He kept his hands in the air. "*Si*?"

"You are under arrest."

Ayala wished he didn't know why they were here, but he did. He committed plenty of crimes through the years and normally got away with each and every one. He didn't kill Angela and had no idea who did. "Wait, *amigos*. You are mistaken. What is this all about?"

They didn't answer. Instead, the policia wrestled him to the ground, cuffed him and led him away.

"You'll be sorry for this." Ayala shouted.

Staffers filled the halls and looked on in stunned disbelief.

They dragged Ayala down the elevator bank and into a waiting police vehicle. Within ten minutes, they locked him up and cuffed him to the chair of a high security interrogation room.

Ayala continued to protest. "Wait. You cannot do this to me. There's no evidence. Stop this now."

The door almost closed when a hand appeared. A young man probably in his twenties stepped inside. Ayala recognized his face, but couldn't recall his name.

"Pepe Ayala?" the man asked.

"Si."

Without another word, the man punched him squarely in the jaw.

Thirty Two

Bene laid flat on his back on an uncomfortable cot in the middle of a room he'd never seen before. He stared up at the thick wooden beams in the ceiling and watched a fan slowly rotate over his head.

He tried to move, but sharp pain ripped through his entire body. His arms stretched over his head. His captors restrained him with thick metal chains around both wrists and his torso. He tried to kick himself free, but found his ankles similarly restrained. Turning his head in each direction, he noticed the room filled with fresh fruit and the smell of fragrant flowers.

A young girl, not more than twelve or so, approached him. She held out food of some kind, but his eyes were too blurry to tell exactly what kind. "*Hola. Te quiere?*"

No, Bene thought. He did not want anything to eat. The pain and anguish of yesterday washed over him and he lost desire for food or anything else.

The girl got closer. "Eat."

"No." He whispered and shook his head violently.

The girl backed away. She seemed frightened of him. She dropped the fruit on the floor and ran away, slamming the door behind her.

Once he knew for sure the little girl was gone, Bene squeezed his fingers together to try and slip free of his restraints. Since yesterday, he'd acquired a sudden will to live so he could personally break the necks of Ricardo and the rest of these people who killed Angela, Jorge and Diego. He did not care about his own life anymore, but while he had breath in his body, he would fight for their sakes and avenge them all.

Benito had no way to fulfill his inner passion for revenge in his current weakened state. The slightest movements caused excruciating pain. He tried to move his legs again, but fell back on the bed, cringing as the door creaked open.

A tall man painted in blue and covered in long white feathers entered his room. "Ah *Quetzalcoatl.* You are awake. I heard you gave my people a difficult time."

Bene stared into the face of the madman. He could not make the features out clearly through the disguise, but the eyes. *He seemed so familiar...*

"Your friends called and called but you didn't answer them." He dangled Bene's phone in front of his face. "Mario Martinez, Stefano Juarez..." He scrolled through the calls. "Several others here too, *amigo*. Seems you are a popular man."

Bene's heart pounded. The thought of this animal going after his family and his last remaining friend made him want to kill this maniac right here and now. He tried to move, imagining he could break free of his shackles, but instead, he moaned and fell back on the bed in agony.

"They say you didn't eat." He made a clicking noise with his tongue. "Now now, Benito. You must keep your strength up. It's no wonder you can barely lift your arm. *Aqui.*" He held out a piece of banana.

Clenching his teeth, Bene moaned his displeasure.

"No?" The evil man tossed the banana over his shoulder. "Suit yourself."

Bene thought about the familiarity of the eyes and the voice when he spoke his name. The feathered man seemed so very familiar. He knew him, but from where?

The captor picked up a papaya. "How about this?"

Bene mumbled through his gag, still refusing to eat.

"What did you say?" The man loosened the tie on his mouth. "Speak up, Benito."

Bene would never give in to any terrorist demands.

"Not going to speak?" The man held up a large hypodermic needle and smiled. "Okay. We will do this your way for now, *Senor Presidente.*"

Bene twisted back and forth on the bed, pulling his arms, kicking his painful legs while the needle came ever closer. "No." He wished he'd kept quiet. He refused to give the maniac the satisfaction of watching him suffer.

The feathered man laughed. "Here you go. You should remember to behave better next time you awaken so you may enjoy your feast."

He struggled against the needle, but soon the flash of pain fell away, and Benito drifted into a dark and unknown place.

Thirty Three

Mario shook the pain out of his right fist. He shouldn't have punched the *Partido La Gente* leader, he knew that, but it felt so good, so long overdue. Ayala was smaller than Mario imagined, older too, which was good. He'd be easier to intimidate. "Do you know me, *Senor* Ayala?"

Ayala licked blood from his bottom lip. "No and you better be glad I don't."

"Mario Martinez."

Ayala's brown skin whitened, his eyes grew slightly wider. "*Martinez*?"

"*Si, Senor* Ayala. I believe you know my sister Angela. Tell me, have you seen her lately?"

"I… don't know about anything," Ayala stammered.

"Angela Martinez, your *numero uno*? She's dead, *Senor*. But you already know that, don't you?" Martinez slapped the crime scene photos on the interrogation room table.

Ayala rubbed his jaw and kept quiet.

"Of course you do. You left these on your desk. The question is, why'd you kill her?"

"I didn't kill anyone." Ayala gazed over Mario's shoulders to the mirrors behind him. "Who's in there? I demand to know who's watching and listening to these ridiculous accusations."

Mario pulled out a chair, took a seat, folded his arms neatly over his center. He leaned back, crossed his legs and rested his feet on the table between them. "That, *Senor* Ayala, is none of your business."

"You stop this right now, Martinez. My people will—"

"Who will what? Kill me? Like you killed Angela?"

Ayala took a breath, unruffled his feathers. "*Nada*. I want to get on with this."

Martinez laughed. "Oh *Senor*, we have all the time in the world around here, in case you didn't know."

Ayala's round face reddened like a balloon about to pop. "You tell me who's behind that window. Now."

"Not until you tell me where you got the photos. Nobody knows about Angela, not the media, not even the government. This situation was kept quiet, so tell me, who gave you these?"

"I want my lawyer before I say another word."

Mario lost his cool.   He lowered his legs and shoved the table forward, hitting Ayala in the gut with the corners. "You think my sister got to call her lawyer? Huh?"

"My lawyers are going to sue your pants off Martinez." Ayala looked into the mirrors, up at the cameras in the corners of the room. "…and whoever put you up to this ridiculous accusation. There is no evidence against me. I've done nothing wrong."

"Prove it." Mario wanted to ask about Bene, but he had specific instructions not to. In the briefing prior to Ayala's detainment, Juarez' advisors said they consider Bene's disappearance a top secret matter of national security. Mario realized everyone in upper government was paranoid about bugs and leaks, not just Benito. Still, he wished Ayala would admit to knowing something.

"You are crazy, *Senor* Martinez, and I suggest you stop this line of questioning this instant, unless you and the city wish to be sued."

Mario took a breath, knowing full well if he didn't calm himself down, the interrogation room doors would likely burst open, and the higher ups would put a stop to his questioning. Then his opportunity to find the truth would be gone forever. "Fine, but while you're waiting for your lawyer, *Senor* Ayala, I want you to you tell me what you know about Angela. Things would go much easier on you if you do." He lifted his arm to strike. "I am authorized to use force, if necessary. I don't want to, but..."

Ayala flinched once Martinez got within an inch of his face. "Alright *amigo*." He laughed nervously.

Mario kept his fist tightened. "Alright what?"

Ayala sighed. "I received the photos yesterday afternoon, late."

"Photos of what?" Martinez needed to get the information on tape.

Ayala sighed. "Angela Martinez' body."

Mario kept his face somber, but inside he felt relieved to finally make progress. "You needed evidence that your orders to kill her were adequately carried out?"

Ayala pounded his fists on the desk. "I told you I didn't have anything to do with this, Martinez. I don't know who sent the pictures. Why would I kill her? I showed these photos to my staff members just this afternoon. Why would I do that if I was guilty?"

Mario realized Ayala had a point. "You were covering yourself."

Ayala rolled his eyes. "From what?"

"From the murder. You showed your staff so they wouldn't find out otherwise and suspect you. The whole thing was staged."

Ayala shook his head. "Ridiculous!"

"Where were you when you received these pictures?"

"In my office."

"Who brought them?"

Ayala shrugged. "I told you, I don't know."

"Don't give me that."

"One of my staff brought them, but he did not know where they came from. I swear."

Mario hated everything this man stood for, but believed Ayala was telling the truth. "Fine. So you are not involved?"

"I am not responsible in any way, shape or form for the death of Angela Martinez. I believe someone nearby is, however, and they might have it in for me too. I'm not sure. I hope not."

Mario stood up and pointed to the photos. "Who did you tell about these?"

Ayala hesitated.

"Who else?" Mario raised his fist to strike.

"No one."

"Liar." Mario tossed his chair to the wall. "Tell me, who."

"My staff only."

"When?"

"This morning,"

This wasn't going anywhere. Time wasting, the clock still ticking, Bene was either dead or being held in some unknown location where he'd already been for a half a day now. Without another word, Mario turned and slammed the door behind him.

Outside, Juarez senior and Rita waited and watched.

Juarez approached, patted Mario on the back. "Good job in there, son."

Mario wasn't sure. He learned remedial interrogation tactics in the military, but always with pretend situations. With such serious matters on the line, he felt like a failure and didn't know what to say.

"Well?" Juarez asked. "Is that it?"

"Si." Mario wiped the sweat from his brow and started to put on his jacket. "I need to get moving."

Juarez grabbed his shoulder. "Wait. You can't go. You said you would help us find Bene by uncovering information from *Partido La Gente*."

Mario clutched the doorknob. "Si, but I was wrong, *Senor*. Ayala is no help."

Juarez put his hand on the door. "You promised me. So far, you've been absolutely no help whatsoever. My son is missing, Martinez, and you and your little impersonation stunt probably cost him his life. We need your help or else we will detain both you and Mr. Ayala until Bene is returned."

Mario felt completely to blame for Benito's disappearance. If he had thought to question things more, Bene would be safe at home right now. "*Senor* Juarez, you watched, you saw Ayala. I got all the information from him I can. That's it. I'm sorry."

Juarez' shoulders sank in defeat. "I suppose you're right."

Mario sighed. "Believe me, I will do anything in my power to find your son, bring justice to those who killed Angela and the other men. I thought Ayala might know something, but in my opinion, he is telling the truth."

"The man's a criminal. What makes you think you can trust him?"

"I never said I trusted him, *Senor*, but I believe him. If I have any chance to find your son alive though, I need to get going now."

"Where will you look first?" Rita asked him.

The thought seemed overwhelming. "I don't know, ma'am. I will retrace the steps, look around the area. To do this, I need your permission and support."

"How do I know I can trust you?" Juarez asked.

"Look into my eyes. You should know all you need to." Mario locked eyes with the elderly Juarez and extended his hand.

Juarez handed him a card from his wallet, then took his hand. "This is my direct line. It forwards to my cell. Call me night or day with any news."

Mario noticed a pad of paper lying on the desk. He wrote his number and tore it off, "Here. My cell. Call anytime, day or night. You have my word, *Senor* Juarez. Bene is a good man and I will do what I can to find him and bring him home safely."

Juarez patted him on the shoulder. "By the way, Martinez."

"*Si?*"

"Where'd you learn your interrogation skills?"

"I didn't. This is my sister and your son we're talking about. I do what I need to do."

"We will pay you handsomely for returning my son. Meanwhile, we already called in extra men from the military and policia."

"I don't do it for money, but I will accept it." Mario remembered what Bene said about trust. Knowing other men would also search for Bene felt both comforting and terrorizing. He hoped these people could be trusted, but for now, he needed to play the game. "Also for this to work, you must agree to a few rules."

Juarez seemed taken aback. "What rules?"

"I prefer to speak only to you and I would also like you to keep my involvement in this situation to yourself for my protection. I do not want my current employer at the *Museo* to know about this, and I want you to personally call Montoya and *Senor*a Sanchez and clear my name. Tell them you are sorry for the mistake. Tell them this is part of the ongoing murder investigation but you secured evidence already clearing me of these crimes. Do not tell them about Bene's disappearance, *Senor*. Based on the discussion Bene and I shared the other day, I am certain he would want this situation kept quiet. If his best friend turned on him, you never know who else might."

Juarez swallowed hard and gripped his hands together. "Si."

"God Bless you, Mario," Rita smiled with tears in her eyes. "Please bring him back to us."

"I will do all I can. You have my word."

***

When the door shut, Juarez turned to Rita. "Do you really think we can trust him?"

She nodded. "Oh yes. If anyone can bring our Bene home to us, it's Mario Martinez."

"How can you be so sure?"

"I have a good feeling about this," Rita said with a smile.

Juarez shrugged. "I hope you're right. Now give me the phone. I need to call the Museo."

Thirty Four

Hundreds of cars and trucks lined up in a gravel field about a quarter mile from the temple. A half delirious Carlos searched the area for the Buick he and Ricardo parked less than thirty minutes earlier.

Men and women who giggled while getting out of their cars fell into hushed silence once they donned their robes and walked across the field to the temple where the drumming and chanting already started.

Once Carlos passed the initial crowds, nobody seemed to care or notice the bloody boy frantically running up and down the rows. He finally found the Buick squeezed tight in between a low-rider and an old Chevy half-ton pickup.

Carlos' hands shook violently as he slid the key in the ignition, praying the stolen car would start and had enough gas to make it home, otherwise he'd be dead for sure. His mother would kill him herself when she got her hands on him. Especially once she found out about El Presidente. At this point, he would rather die by his mother's hand than out here in who-knows-where. She might understand once he explained the older boys who told him how much money he could make by joining them. His mother always complained about not having enough. He only wanted to help.

He backed out, accidentally scraping the car against the side of the pickup. He cringed to think what the pickup owner would do to him if he got caught.

Carlos didn't have much experience driving. Today he drove more miles than he ever had in his life. Backing out of cramped spaces wasn't his strong suit, not yet anyway.

He pulled out, careful not to hit anyone else, and slowly inched between the rows of cars until he pulled out to the main road he and Ricardo used to get here. At the intersection, he felt so nervous, he wondered which way to turn at first, until he noticed the long line of cars coming from his left. *That way.* The other direction seemed to go further out into nowhere. He waited for an opening, and pulled out on the two lane highway.

The road stretched on for what seemed like forever, and Carlos worried he might not find his way back to the city. When he eventually found another intersection and overpass, he believed luck was on his side when several cars pulled off the road from his left. He crossed the bridge and noticed a small dented sign saying *Ciudad Mexico*. He remembered this four lane road and turned.

He dabbed the last fresh white towel on his face, drenching it in red. *It's okay. No need to panic about the blood.* Soon he would be home with his mother and everything would be alright.

Thirty Five

Outside the policia station, Mario turned on his cell.. It buzzed with a new message. He listened to his mother crying and telling him how worried she was about him. He hated to stop for the day with Bene still out there somewhere, but with the sun nearly gone, he figured he needed to go see his poor mother again, sooner, rather than later. He dialed.

She answered on the first ring. "Mario. When are you coming home?"

"I'm on my way now, Mama."
***

An hour later, Mario sat at the old kitchen table across from his mother and buried his face in his hands. Beyond exhausted, he needed a break in the case. *Maybe tomorrow.*

"Tell me what's going on." His mother rubbed his shoulders and took a seat across from him.

He didn't know where to begin. Too much information in his mother's case would be far worse than giving her vague details. "They hired me to help with the investigation into Angela's death, look into some things."

She made the sign of the cross over her heart. "What things, Mario?"

He knew he couldn't tell his mother about the Presidente. Their family was lucky the media hadn't already caught wind of it. "I can't say, mama. They like my military training and the fact I can be trusted, so they asked me to poke around, ask a few questions, that's all."

She grabbed his sleeve. "Is it dangerous? Please tell me it isn't."

He knew her looks. His mother had the same expression as when he skinned a knee or bruised his arm playing football. "No, mama. It isn't. It will be okay."

His mother had that worried look on her face with good reason. Since Angela's death her fears were now grounded in reality. "Mario…tell me the truth."

He sighed. He never lied to his mother, but he needed to keep her from worrying herself to death. "I'm careful. My problem is this is a murder case, so of course there are mean people in this world, you know that, but it's what I must do."

"Promise you won't do anything dangerous."

He rolled his eyes. "Mama…"

" Promise."

"I will do my best to be safe, but I cannot make a promise unless I know I can keep it."

His mother sobbed. "I can't lose both my babies."

Mario wished his poor mother would stop her panicking. That was her nature, though. Always a worrier. "Shhh. Mama, please. The people who hired me are going to pay me well to do this job. We need the money right now."

"No, I don't want it, none of it. You keep it. You have a home of your own. I've got plenty here."

For the first time in two days, Mario remembered he hadn't seen the inside of his tiny house since he showed up for work two days ago and found his sister dead. None of that mattered to him anymore. "Don't be ridiculous. This is our money. You and me are all we have left." Tears filled his eyes. "I will take care of you now." They never spoke of his father anymore. He'd been gone a long time, but the pain still lingered under the surface and was exasperated now with Angela gone too.

His mother sniffled. "Si, which is why I cannot have you out there getting yourself killed. Tell them to find someone else to do this job. We don't need their money."

On one hand, Mario wished he could get out for his mother's sake, but they both knew he was in way too deep. "I can't. This is your daughter we're talking about, my sister. I will find these people and make them pay for what they've done to our family. Justice will prevail."

"Si, I hope you are right."

"What about Angela? What about the funeral arrangements? I cannot do it all myself."

Mario knew his mother would not wait long before bringing this sore subject up again. He was actually surprised she hadn't tried to find his sister's body earlier in the day, but from the looks of her ragged state of mind, she barely had the strength to eat or take a shower, let alone fight her way into the city. "Si, I know."

"You haven't given me any details about her. I want to see her and you've said nothing. Tomorrow you will take me, Mario. She needs a proper burial." She sniffed. "I spoke to Father Ortiz and he wants to know when she will be transferred to the funeral home here."

God how he wished his mother would drop it, but he knew she never would, and he didn't blame her. Any parent would want this closure. Now that the family priest was involved, he knew he had no choice but to come clean. "Mama…"

"*Si?*"

Mario sighed. He didn't want to tell his poor mother about the condition of Angela's body, let alone the fact that she disappeared right out from under everyone's eyes, but she gave him no choice. "I did not want to tell you this…"

"Que? What could be any worse than what you told me yesterday, Mario? Huh? Ineed to see my baby."

"This is the problem. Angela disappeared."

His mother scowled. "Que? What do you mean?"

Mario gulped. "Well I wanted to bring her back to you before now, but someone stole her body from the Eagle Chamber right after the murder. I am doing my best to find her and bring her—"

"Agh." His mother screamed at the top of her lungs. "Tell me this isn't so."

"Please, Mama." Mario yelled even though he didn't want to. If he couldn't keep his cool around here, nobody could. "I am doing everything I can to bring her home. This is why I agreed to work for the investigators because I must find her."

A faint glimmer of hope shone in her aging eyes. "Are you sure she is dead?"

Tears fell down his cheeks. "Si, I saw her myself. I found her." The image washed through the interior of his mind again. He pressed his eyes closed, hoping to squeeze it out. "When I went to get the policia, I came back, but her body disappeared. I didn't want to tell you. I know you're upset…"

His mother slapped him hard across the face and cried louder. "Why?"

The sting actually helped ease the pain of his heart. "I am sorry. I wanted to find her before now but I have no clues, nowhere to look. I am scared. And there is more I haven't been able to tell you about…"

"Oh Mario. I am so sorry." She brushed her hand on the red spot on his cheek. "I did not mean this is your fault."

"I know."

Outside the door, the sound of screaming caused them both to stop and look.

A loud knock on the door interrupted the conversation and they both jumped to their feet.

Mario pushed his mother aside, drew his gun. "Shhh. Stay back."

"What are you doing?"

He pressed his fingers to his lips and whispered. "Get under the table, Mama. Now."

She d huddled behind one of the kitchen chairs.

"Who's there?" Mario swung the door open and stepped outside, gun drawn.

The petite neighbor lady stood on his mother's porch. With swollen eyes and fresh tears, she threw up her hands. "Don't shoot."

"Who are you?" Mario kept his gun drawn.

"Mario. Stop. This is Sylvia from next door."

He watched her for a moment and then lowered the gun. "I'm sorry. Please, come in."

"Oh thank God." Sylvia cried. "Help me. My son is missing."

Thirty Six

"Stefano, *por favor*. What's wrong, *amigo*?"
After a second evening of drinking alone, Stefano Juarez Senior knew he must confide in the one and only friend he'd ever been able to rely on throughout the years. He picked up the phone and dialed.

Berto Mendoza was there for him when his wife died, supported him while he raised Bene as a single father, and now in the most difficult chapter of them all. He worried Bene might fall into the hands of some sick terrorists and he might never see him again. He knew better but he had to talk to someone, and he had nobody else to turn to.

Despite national security warnings, Juarez needed his friend more than ever. He never meant to call Berto tonight, and certainly didn't want to break down in sobs on the telephone, but here they were again, two old friends comforting each other in their darkest hours. "Berto..."

"Amigo. Do you need me to come over there? What is wrong, my friend?"

Juarez took a deep breath, tried to stop the tremor in his voice. "Berto, something terrible happened."

"What is it, por favor?"

"It's Bene...someone kidnapped him, possibly killed him."

"No."

"*Si* and I don't know what to do. Please pray for us."

"*Que*? How did this happen?" Berto asked.

In between sobs, Juarez explained everything from Angela's death to Bene's disappearance and the murder of two of his best friends. "Only Ricardo hasn't been found. I pray he is with Bene, even if they got to him too, I must believe he is helping him somehow."

Berto sighed. "I don't know what to say, *amigo*. I will pray the Rosary for you this very night."

"*Gracias.*"

"What else can I do, Stefano? Do you need my help in any other way?"

Juarez sighed. "Bene apparently spoke to Angela's brother Mario Martinez before he disappeared. He trusted the kid and he is very good. We hired him to look into this. I hope he can help, but I am not sure yet. He's too young, has no experience."

"I pray he can, *amigo*," Berto said. "I pray he can."
***

In a darkened room illuminated only by the flame of a single candle, Benito attempted to lift his head and open his eyes, but the pain felt too intense., His brain swam around in a pool of dazed awareness. He tried to speak, but realized it sounded more like mumbling than any intelligent form of communication.

The young girl who offered him food earlier crossed the room and stood over his bed. "*Hola.* Drink, *por favor.* I am told you must drink. Please…" She reached her hand under the back of his head, tilting it forward and dipped a spoon in a bowl, inching it toward his mouth.

Bene mumbled louder. He didn't want this. It tasted bitter, like a root, and he felt sure it would only make his mind more incapable of doing anything but lying here. He remembered Angela like a far off distant dream. Closer still were memories of the fresh bodies of his best friends and the Ricardo who turned on them all. Bene wanted to break Ricardo's skull open. In his mind, he lurched forward and roared in rage at the thought, but in reality, he could barely move his head and the loud sounds he made seconds before grew quieter now, his mind became ever weary.

"Don't be afraid," the girl said. "We want to take care of you and feed you well. All you need to do is relax and everything will be okay." She scraped the final spoonfuls of the concoction into his mouth. "There you go. You will be all better after you sleep."

Bene drifted out of the room again, and wondered if the girl knew what she was doing to him. He wanted to believe her innocence. She was merely a pawn in the evil scheme. His eyelids pressed together before he could consider this further, and he drifted away once again.

***

On a hill in a northern neighborhood of Mexico City, a man waited in a parked El Dorado, looking out his binoculars at a group of homes when his cell phone rang. "*Hola?*"

"We have a problem," said the voice.

"Oh?"

"Si. We need you to take care of it tonight."

The man listened intently while the voice described the exact nature of the problem. "Okay. I will tend to it."

"*Gracias.*" The line went dead.

Thirty Seven

Sylvia Ortiz lived next door to Elsa Martinez for the past twenty years. A single parent whose oldest kids were already grown and gone, Sylvia ran next door to find one of the only friends she could count on in times like these. She stood on the porch until Elsa's son lowered his weapon.

"Come inside, Sylvia," Mario said. "Please take a seat."

She walked inside the cramped living room and paced around in front of the TV. "I'm sorry to bother you, but I don't know what to do. My youngest Carlos disappeared. I don't know who else to call."

"Are you sure?" Mario asked.

Sylvia wiped her tears. "I looked in his bedroom and found his suitcase missing."

"He might be over at a friend's house," Elsa offered.

"No. I called his friends but he isn't there either, and now I find this." Sylvia held up an old pillowcase stained with blood.

Mario took it and held it up to the light. "When did you last see him?"

"Two days ago in the morning before he went to school." Sylvia noticed Elsa's swollen eyes and distressed look. "What's wrong?"

Elsa's eyes filled with tears. "My Angela. She is dead."

Sylvia nearly collapsed at the news. "No."

Elsa sniffled. "*Si*."

Sylvia put an arm around her friend. "Please tell me this is a mistake."

Mario felt bad. Normally he would jump to help her, but with all going on and his commitment to Benito and his family and his determination to find Angela's killers, he was stretched to his limits. "We want to help you, Sylvia. I'll help you, it's just my hands are full at the moment, but somehow we will find Carlos. I promise. We will help each other."

Sylvia fell to her knees and cried. "God help us all."
***

Carlos felt relieved when he finally pulled on to his street and drove slowly up the hill toward his house. He hoped his mother wasn't home from work yet so he could be there when she arrived and explain what happened.

Closer to his house, he noticed the living room lights were still out. Good. This would give him time. Once his mother came home, he would tell her all about *El Presidente* and get someone to go out there and help him.

Carlos still didn't know the name of the temple and he never heard anyone call it by name, but he could take someone there once he felt better. Right now, his bleeding made him a little dizzy, but by tomorrow, he would feel well enough to lead the authorities to Benito.

He parked the Buick on the street. In his panic, he parked a foot away from the curb. He knew he should do better, but not now. He didn't feel too good and his t-shirt was soaked in blood. He stumbled up the gravel yard toward the door.

A tall man dressed in a pale colored linen jacket, a hat and dark sunglasses appeared from behind a wooden beam on the porch. "*Hola.*"

"*Ho..*" Before Carlos could finish his greeting, the man lunged forward and pierced a sharp object through his gut. He heard the tear of his shirt as the tip of the blade stuck out his back.

The man jerked the knife out and walked off. "*Adios amigo*. See you in hell."

Carlos fought to get his breath. He clutched his stomach, tried his front door. It was locked. He turned around and saw the man get into a car and speed away and noticed the lights on at his next door neighbor's house.

His mother would be furious, but he needed help right now. He stumbled through the yard, tripping over a prickly pear and staggered to the neighbor's porch, pounding on the door. Before anyone answered, he fell against the door and hit his head.

***

Mario jumped when he heard the knock at the door. "Shhhh." He pushed his mother and Sylvia back toward the kitchen and whispered. "Stay back you two. Get down." He drew his gun. "Who's there?"

Nobody answered. He put his ear to the door and heard a strange thud.

Mario's eyes ran down the door and a crimson pool seeped under the crack and trickled on her old linoleum floor. "Stay back and get down," he told the women.

He stood behind the door, carefully cracked it open, stunned when the near lifeless body of a boy fell into his mother's kitchen.

"Carlos." Sylvia Ortiz screamed bloody murder, nearly piercing Mario's eardrums. "Carlos." She fell to her knees.

"Get back." Mario lifted his revolver and ran to the door in time to see the black El Dorado speed away. "Listen. Call the ambulance, Mama. Now."

His mother ran waving her arms and crying from the kitchen. "*Si.*"

Mario flipped the boy over and saw the blood gurgling from the sides of his mouth. "Who did this to you Carlos? Please. Tell me."

Carlos whispered. "*El Presidente.*"

Barely able to hear him, Mario put his ear up to the boy's mouth. "*Que?*"

"*El Presidente.*"

Adrenaline rushed through Mario's veins. "What? You saw *El Presidente*?"

"*Si…*"

"Where?"

"Temple Azteca…"

Dear God! Mario couldn't believe he finally had the first evidence of the fact that Benito had indeed been kidnapped. "Which temple?" He pressed the boy's wound with his hands. "Mama, hurry. Towels. Bring me towels, sheets. Anything. Fast. I've got to stop his bleeding."

Elsa was busy on the phone. She tried to explain the situation to the police, but blubbered so much they might not have heard the address. Once she hung up, she ran to the drawers and threw towels at her son.

Sylvia screamed and cried, hysterically trying to run her fingers through Carlos' hair. "Oh my baby. Please. Oh no."

"Sylvia." Mario snapped. "Please calm down. Listen." He turned back to Carlos, whose voice grew ever fainter.

He patted the boy's cheeks, hoping to revive him. "Carlos. Stay with me. Open your eyes. Look at me."

Carlos' eyes rolled back in his head. He mumbled something.

Mario pulled his hands back from the bloody sides of the boy's head and cringed at the sight of his missing earlobe. "Carlos. Listen to me. You will be alright. Now tell me where you saw *El Presidente*?"

Carlos didn't look good. "Templo…"

"Si, but which one?"

"*Yo no...*"

"You don't know?" Mario asked.

Before he could answer, Carlos' whole body went limp and he lost consciousness.

"Stop." Sylvia screamed. "Can't you see you're killing him with these questions?"

"Sylvia, calm down. We all need to remain calm." Mario said. "Mama. Did you call the ambulance?"

Elsa shook and sniffed. "*Si*. They are coming."

Mario couldn't believe how close to home these monsters came tonight. Apparently someone sent a message through his neighbor's son, but who?

Sylvia held her son's hand and brushed her fingers through his hair while they waited for the paramedics to arrive. "Carlos, it's mama. Please be strong, baby."

Poor Sylvia. Mario thanked God his own mother didn't see her daughter die. Judging from the severity of Carlos' wounds, if help didn't arrive soon, he wasn't long for the world. He hoped Carlos would regain consciousness and tell him what happened to Bene. *God I hope they get here on time.*

Thirty Eight

The feathered man wiped his makeup off, placed his ceremonial items on the altar where they would remain until tomorrow and prepared to step in the shower when his phone rang. "*Hola.*"

"It is done."

"Finished?"

"*Si.*"

"Exactly as I told you?"

"*Si.*"

"And the other?"

"I'm on my way there now."

"Remember, just a scare, nothing more."

"*Si.*"

"*Excellente.*" Without another word, he hung up and stepped into the shower, washing off the sins of the masses who gathered today. Tomorrow his moment of triumph would arrive. The gods would be pleased.

***

Right around midnight, Mario paced the halls outside the doors of the operating room where Carlos underwent emergency surgery. Thankfully the boy made it to the hospital alive, and by the grace of God, he might live to tell about this. He wished Carlos told him where he saw Bene, but at least he knew Bene was still alive. A glimmer of hope, no matter how small, seemed better than nothing.

His mother embraced Sylvia in the far corner of the waiting room where they talked a mile a minute.

A million thoughts rushed through Mario's mind. First and foremost the fact that somebody close to his family happened to see Bene alive. He couldn't get over how close to home the killers came tonight. They must be watching his every move. He couldn't understand why these maniacs seemed so set against destroying his life. They obviously knew him personally and planned to attack him and his family at their very core. This had something to do with the entire Martinez family, rather than Angela alone. The fact Benito was involved made it all the more complex, but what if he was under attack because of them, and not the other way around? So many thoughts filled his mind. He wanted to know why so he could find a way to stop these madmen before any more innocent blood was shed.

Mario didn't recall much about his father since he left when he was just a boy. From what Elsa said, the man was a loser, but surely his indiscretions weren't enough to warrant such violence. No. It must be something else, but what?

For now, Bene was alive and being held at an Aztec temple. Thank God. He wished he could go search for him tonight, but his mother and Sylvia could not be left alone. Mexican hospitals were dangerous places any time of day, especially at night when they criminals gunned down in bad drug deals filled up emergency rooms. Mario worried about one other person. He picked up his cell and made a call.

**

Juarez Senior shot up in bed when his telephone rang. He clicked on the light and fumbled for it on his bedside table. "*Hola.*"

"*Senor* Juarez? It's Mario Martinez."

Juarez panicked, leapt out of bed and paced the floors. "Martinez? Did you hear from Bene?"

"*Si, Senor.* My neighbor's son was stabbed tonight and just before he collapsed, he said he saw Bene alive."

"Oh thank God. Do you have him now? Where is he?"

"That's the problem. He is only a child, *Senor*, and went unconscious before I could get all the details. I am in the emergency room now. He's undergoing surgery."

Juarez heard nothing Mario said except that Benito was alive out there somewhere. "Did he tell you where Bene is at?"

"In an Aztec Temple, but I'm not sure which one. The boy lost consciousness before I could get any details."

"Find out," Juarez barked.

"I hope I can. I'm not sure the boy's going to make it, *Senor*. His injuries are severe."

Juarez braced himself against the back of his couch. "He has to pull though. Without him, we might never find my son."

"I understand your frustration, but for now, we need to pray for this boy, and hope he will wake up in time to lead us to Benito. He is our best hope, our only hope so far."

"You're right, Martinez." Juarez took a deep breath, calmed himself. "I'm sorry. This is good news. Bene is still alive, there is hope."

"*Si.*"

Just then, a loud blasting sound hurled through Juarez' home and the glass window in his living room crashed to the carpet. He ducked, shouted. "Agh!"

"Did I hear a gunshot?" Mario asked. "*Senor* Juarez? *Senor*? Are you there? Are you okay?"

Juarez stood up, brushed shards of glass from his pant legs. "Si, someone just put a bullet through my front window."

"Get on the floor, lay down. Tell me where you are. I'm on my way."

Outside, car tires screeched and Juarez saw a car speeding away. "That won't be necessary. They're gone."

***

"But *Senor* Juarez…" Mario glanced over at his mother and Sylvia and realized he would have to take them with him. With everything happening tonight there was no way he would let the two of them out of his sight.

"I said no and I mean it. I am afraid if you try to come here, they may kill you and I will never get my Bene back."

"*Si*, but what about you?"

"I'll be fine."

"Are your guards on duty tonight?"

"No. Only at special events."

"Did you happen to see the car?"

"*Si*. An El Dorado."

Mario shivered. "What color?"

"Dark blue, maybe black."

"I saw the same car in my neighborhood speeding away right after the boy got shot. This is personal, *Senor* Juarez. I am afraid none of us are safe any longer. Meet me in your office first thing in the morning."

"I'll have some of my men—"

"No," he snapped. "No help. I'll be there at dawn." Mario hung up the phone and spun around.

A reporter in a tight skirt and high heels stuck her microphone in his face. "*Hola, Senor*. What do you know about tonight's shooting?"

Great. Just what they needed. It was only a matter of time before this mess would be all over the TV.

She smiled. "*Mi nombre es* Bella Perez…"

"Si, I know who you are, *Senorita*." Mario knew Bella, the top tabloid television reporter in the city, known for conveniently skewing facts when necessary to get a scoop.

Tonight Bella dressed like she always did on TV- skin tight hot pink suit, three inch high snakeskin textured heels and fingernails longer than coat hooks. Apparently flattered he recognized her, she batted her eyes and leaned forward to offer him a special view. "Oh, *gracias*."

Mario pretended not to notice the cleavage and glanced over Bella's shoulder at his mother and Sylvia, who held hands and chattered away at each other. "I can't talk to you right now. Excuse me." He started to walk away.

Bella ran in front of him and held the microphone in front of his mouth while a camera rolled behind her. "Please, my story is due. Do you know the boy in the surgery now? I heard he was stabbed. Any comment?"

Surely she was smart enough to figure things out without his help. Mario wasn't about to compromise his investigation regardless of how sexy she looked. "I know nothing. *Buenos noches*." He turned and walked away without another word.

DAY THREE

Thirty Nine

Bene felt woozy. He had some idea of the fact he'd been slipping in and out of consciousness for who knew how long, but when he heard the voices speaking to him, he still found he could not move a muscle.

"Good morning, *Quetzalcoatl*."

Bene immediately recognized the familiar voice he could not yet place. He vaguely remembered his captor from the other day, and hoped this time, if he held completely still and didn't try to fight, the man would not administer any more needles. He decided to be silent too. Last time, when he moved around and struggled, it only made matters worse. He needed to keep his senses about him if he ever hoped to escape.

"I said good morning, *Quetzalcoatl*," the tormentor repeated.

Bene wondered what might happen if he ignored his captor completely. He might become angry. He cracked his eyelids open just slightly enough to feel the sting of the morning sun. He expected to see the same blue faced man, but now instead, he wore a heavy wooden mask, similar to that of an ancient Aztec god Bene could not quite place because of his diminished mental faculties.

The red face and exaggerated mouth filled with teeth was accentuated by a full headdress of peacock feathers. On the man's chest, Bene noticed several deep black tattoos hidden behind multiple strands of bulky turquoise beads. His weathered hand gripped a wooden staff tipped by a black obsidian blade similar to those on display in the best anthropology museums in Mexico. Bene tried not to register his fear. He looked directly into the eyeholes on the mask and kept still.

The man leaned forward until his beads brushed Bene's chest. "That's it, *Quetzalcoatl*. Are you ready for tonight?"

Why is he calling me that? Bene made no verbal acknowledgement whatsoever. Instead, he closed his eyes and used his remaining strength for listening. Oh how he wished he could get out of his mind, get up, and do something about the torture being inflicted on who knew how many nameless, faceless young people. When he tried to concentrate on his arm, see if he could move at all, he realized his restraints were no longer limited to the shackles and chains that bound him. Now, his own lack of brain power needed to connect his physical and mental self together were long gone.

"*Quetzalcoatl?* Are you ready to be sacrificed by the Hummingbird to the Left? I am *Huitzilopochtli*, the Hummingbird incarnate, you know?"

This sounded like crazy talk. Bene had no idea what the man was talking about, but regardless, he wasn't afraid to die. He already resigned himself to death after he saw Angela's pictures and discovered the bloody bodies of his best friends in the alley. He only wished he could find a way to stop these people from harming anyone else.

This must be a cult of some kind. Bene did not possess the mental energy reserves to figure out what kind and why they seemed bent on such incredible levels of destruction.

With his mind half gone and his body restrained from drugs and metal braces, he decided he would fight only if and when he could make a real impact. His time for rebellion was coming soon.

"Speak up, *Quetzalcoatl*." The man shoved him.

Bene wished the man would stop calling him that. *If only the fog in my mind would clear.*

"He hasn't moved all night, *Senor*."

Bene heard the voice of the young girl, who he figured must be standing somewhere off to the side of the bed, or near the door. His head was too heavy to move though.

"Oh? And how do you know that, young lady?" the feathered man asked.

"I was told to sit here and watch him and I did," she replied.

"Make sure to limit his *pulque* today. We will give him more before we leave for the ceremony. We want him stumbling, but he must be able to walk to the altar."

"*Si Senor*." Strangely, the girl's tone suggested the masked man didn't scare her.

Bene cracked open his eyes and saw the girl at the foot of his bed. *If only I could get through to her...*

The masked man leaned down over him and pointed a stone knife directly at his heart. "Tonight you and I will meet for the final battle. Rest well, *Quetzalcoatl*. This day will be your last."

Forty

As promised, Mario arrived at the Palacio right at dawn. Flanks of Presidential guards cleared a path for him and he made his way upstairs and walked down the corridor where he met with Bene only two days ago. So much happened since then, and so many more horrific things would surely take place if he didn't hurry and find Benito Juarez.

"Martinez. Come in."

"*Senor* Juarez. Good morning."

"How is the boy? Did he make it?"

Mario was relieved to be able to report some good news in the midst of all the tragedy. "*Si*. He's not out of the woods yet, but doctors do believe he will live. He had a very close call though."

"Did he say anything yet about Bene?"

Mario shook his head. "I'm afraid not, *Senor*. I checked again before coming here, and he is still not awake yet."

"Keep an eye on him."

"Si, I will. And you? No further trouble last night?"

"No. I don't care about me. " Juarez paced in front of Bene's. "What are we going to do about Benito? I can't understand why these people haven't called to demand money. I am prepared to pay whatever they ask, do whatever they want."

Gut instinct told Mario this crime was far more complex. "*Senor*, they do not want your money."

Juarez laughed nervously. "What are you talking about, Martinez? Of course they do. Isn't that what all kidnappers want? Money?"

Mario sighed. "I wish it was that simple, *Senor*. You do not understand who we are dealing with. They tore my sister's heart out, ripped Bene's friends to shreds and sliced the earlobes from a thirteen year old boy before leaving him for dead."

"Yes, but I have enough money for all of that, maybe more."

"I appreciate that, but it won't work. They want something money can't buy. Revenge. Although I don't understand what this vengeance is about yet, *Senor*, and right now, it doesn't matter. Once we get Bene returned safely, we can rest. Meanwhile, so you can see the brutality of what we are dealing with, I brought this." Mario lay the security camera tape on the desk, gestured to a nearby TV and video player. "Please, take a look."

Juarez popped the tape into the recorder and pushed play. The video showed the stooped over elderly woman sitting on a bench being hit on the head with an obsidian topped war club, and dragged out a door into a restricted area. "Good Lord. Where did you get this?"

"I removed it from the security camera in the *museo* the other day." Mario wanted to remind Juarez about the day they unnecessarily detained him, but didn't want to open up a sore subject.

Juarez squinted and stepped closer to the TV. "My God! That club looks like a museum artifact."

"*Si*. These are sick individuals, *Senor* Juarez. They kill helpless old ladies, children. They kill with no remorse. If they wanted your money, they would have already asked. I need to get going now if I will find Bene."

"Where will you go? Where will you look?"

"Before he lost consciousness, Carlos the young boy, told me Bene is at an Aztec temple. I will need a list of all the temples in the area. I will look at each of them."

"There are only a few around here. Templo Mayor of course, and Grand Temple in Las *Plaza de las Tres Culturas*...a few others, although I'm afraid I don't know all the names from memory."

"Me neither."

Juarez pounded his fists on the desk. "Damn it. Bene has been gone for three days. What are we going to do?"

"I will search the temples myself."

"You need someone to help you. I can call..."

"No. I told you. Someone close is leaking information. We must keep this quiet."

"Fine. I will come with you myself."

"No *Senor*. You are too important to Mexico. Stay here. You are second in command. If something happens..."

"Nothing will happen to my son if you get busy and find him."

Mario lowered his eyes in shame. Juarez was right. Benito should have come home by now. "I'm doing my best."

Juarez clutched his forehead. "I'm sorry. I'm losing my mind."

"Please stay in this office today. Do not go out. It's not safe. Is *Senora* Rita coming in to work today?"

"*Si.*"

"She should stay here too. I will go to the temples and get back to you once I know anything."

"Which will you visit first?"

"*Yo no se*. I will start with the closest ones first, then I will move farther outside the city center. First, I will need to go get a map, unless you have one here."

"No, I don't." Juarez glanced around.

"I need to get going then. I'll check them all if necessary."

"Won't you need protection?"

Mario slapped his gun belt. "I have all the protection I need here." He pulled his cross out from under his shirt. "And here."

Forty One

Bene smelled the sweet scent of incense and felt a tug at his chest. He cracked open his eyes and saw the girl lighting a large piece of copal amber incense and waving it over his body.

She sat it down and began tearing at his clothes, ripping his shirt to shreds.

Bene mumbled at her. He wanted to speak to her and hopefully talk her out of all this, but he garbled his words.

She seemed to understand him. "This is the purification. Hold still. I need to bathe and purify you."

He tried to lift his arms, but they didn't work.

The girl dabbed his chest with a wet sponge, wiped the dirt and sweat from his forehead.

At first, the water felt refreshing, until he felt the sting of hot water seeping down into his open cuts. He gritted his teeth and cringed.

She laid the sponge down and continued her ritual, running incense over him and chanting in a language he could not understand. She placed the items on a nearby table and lifted the cup to his mouth. "Drink."

He moaned his displeasure, tried to knock it from her hands. He couldn't help but wonder what might happen to her if he refused, so he quieted down and allowed it. The liquid dribbled down his face, and Bene realized his lips didn't work any better than any other part of him.

She wiped the excess off his chin, picked up the spoon like before. "There you are."

He tasted the same bitter mixture as before. It rushed down the back of his throat, numbing his windpipe as it traveled into his stomach. This batch seemed far stronger than previous concoctions.

Heavy footsteps and a deep male voice interrupted the silence. "Is he taking the preparations?"

Bene turned his head slightly and saw the same man again, only now, his mask was off, and his face was painted red, yellow, white and black. He wore a less elaborate headdress, this one made of leather and beads. The voice still echoed to a deep part of his mind, but with his face all covered, Benito still had no recollection of his identity.

"*Si*," the girl answered.

"*Bueno*, then paint him with this once he finishes. Make him look like the picture I showed you the other day, *comprende?*" The man loomed over Bene's bed. "Only a few more hours, *Quetzalcoatl*. Soon you will be one with the spirit."

Too woozy to panic about his impending doom, by the time he tasted a few more drops of the hallucinogenic drink, Bene passed out cold.

Forty Two

S tanding outside the door to the Templo Mayor Museo, Mario's stomach tied in a knot. He wondered if Juarez kept his word about calling his employer. Even if the situation was properly cleared up, he still wondered how he would be received after his detainment yesterday morning and the embarrassment it caused *Senora* Sanchez.

Juarez supposedly handled it, so Mario assumed he kept his word. With all the events of the past twenty four hours, he forgot to ask Juarez how it went. It didn't matter. He needed the list of Aztec sites. He walked through the front door and into the lobby, surprised nobody stopped him in his civilian clothes.

"*Hola* Mario." Juan, another guard he'd met only a time or two, stood in the lobby.

Mario slapped Juan on the back. "*Que pasa*? I am off today but I need to see *Senora* Sanchez. Is she here?"

He pointed toward the offices. "*Si*, in the back."

"Gracias." He walked past the exhibits and around the corner until he reached her office and gently knocked on her door. "*Hola, Senora* Sanchez."

Amelia Sanchez sat behind her desk, head bowed, filling out paperwork. She jumped when she saw him. "Mario. *Hola.* You're still off today, si?"

"*Si*, but I need your help with some research."

Sanchez gestured to the chair. "Come in, have a seat."

He pulled out the metal chair, scraping the legs against the tile. "I need to know where the different Aztec sights are in and around the city."

Sanchez dropped her pencil on the desk, pulled off her glasses. "Why?"

"I believe people might be in danger from the same men who killed my sister. I want to look around and see what I can find. Maybe nothing, but I need to look. Also, I'd like to check the door to the restricted area, see if it goes somewhere. I think it might be a vulnerable spot where the killers gained access to the *museo*."

Sanchez sighed. "Mario, look, I know your sister's death is horrible for you and your family, but you must let this go. It won't do any good to run around town trying to find things that don't actually exist. The policia were here for the past two days and believe me, everything is under control. You would be better off going home, helping your family, at least until they find whoever did this. I told you the other day to take off as much time as you need, and I meant it. Go home, Mario, please." She picked up her pencil and began reading again.

Mario scooted his chair closer to her desk. "I can't."

She tapped her pencil on her desk and sighed. "I told you, the policia are investigating. It will all work out, I promise. Now go."

"What about the restricted area?"

"It says restricted for a reason, now go."

"But it might lead somewhere. I have to find out, *Senora*."

"There's nothing down there except for a bunch of electrical boxes and power transformers to run our Museo."

"So you've been in there?"

Sanchez sighed. "Will you please leave?"

"What would you do if your sister was murdered? Wouldn't you check every detail until you found justice?"

"Mario…"

"My sister's body is missing, *Senora*. What am I supposed to tell my mother?"

Her voice got louder. "Mario, I…"

"Please. I need to get into that door."

She yelled. "Mario. I can't help you, and I don't know why you're obsessing over a supply closet. I'm begging you, go home."

Good. He was getting under her skin. Mario knew he had to be careful about what he told Sanchez, but he would not rest until he gained access inside the restricted area. "I am here now."

Sanchez raised her voice. "If you were a janitor, a construction worker, an electrician, fine, you could look in the door, but we do not open it for just anyone."

He realized he needed to stop before he pressed his luck and Sanchez had security kick him out. "Okay, but do you have a map of some of the temple sites around here? I'll take a quick look at those, and then I promise, I will go home and help my mother."

Sanchez reached into a desk drawer and pulled out one of the free city maps they handed to tourists. "Here. This is what I would use.   There are several places near the *Zocalo* and *Plaza de la Tres Culturas*. Go look, then go home."

Mario stuffed the map in his pocket. "*Gracias*, I will. Oh and *Senora*?"

"*Si*?"

"About what happened yesterday morning…"

"*Senor* Juarez called over here to say his men were out of line and made a horrible mistake. It's forgotten. I'm just sorry you're going through all of this right now. It makes a bad situation even worse which is one reason why I am asking you to take the time and go home."

"*Si...gracias.*"

"Go home and stay there, okay? At least until next week."

"*Si, adios.*" Mario turned to go and ran into Montoya right outside the office, nearly knocking a cup of coffee out of his hand in the process. "Pardon me."

"Martinez? What are you doing here?" Montoya asked.

"I...uh...Checking with *Senora* Sanchez to make sure things are cleared up after what happened yesterday."

"They are, go home," Montoya said.

That was his cue to leave. Mario couldn't risk enflaming either of them today.

***

Montoya walked into Sanchez' office and closed the door behind him. "What was that all about?"

"Nothing."

"Really? Then why is he holding a map?"

"He wants to look around at some sites, make sure there isn't any evidence anywhere," she sighed. "And he really wants access to the restricted area."

Montoya pointed his finger toward the door. "You keep him out of this building until I say so, and whatever you do, don't let him anywhere near that door downstairs, understood?"

"*Si, Senor* Montoya."

Forty Three

J uarez picked up the ringing phone in his office. "*Hola*?"

"Stefano? *Que pasa*? I've been worried about you after we talked last night. Is everything okay? Did you find your son?"

Juarez felt relieved to hear Berto's voice. "No, but things are better, at least."

"Oh?"

"*Si*, we got a lead. Bene is still alive."

"Thank God. Where is he?"

"I don't know. He's apparently being held at a temple someplace, although we do not know the location."

"Really? How did you find that out?"

"A boy got stabbed last night. He says he saw Bene."

"Really? Where?"

"*Yo no se*. He just got out of surgery and couldn't tell us yet. We're hoping to talk to him once he wakes up."

"This is a miracle." Berto said.

"Si, *amigo*, I am hoping we can find him now before it's too late. I sent our man Martinez to try and find him."

"*Muy bueno*," Berto said. "I will pray for you."

"*Gracias*. We need all the prayer we can get."

***

The man who believed he was the embodiment of *Huitzilopochtli* stared down at Mexico's youngest *Presidente* and studied him carefully. His pale white skin, dark hair and beard only further solidified the fact that Benito Juarez was indeed the returned god, *Quetzalcoatl*. Not since the days of Cortez had any mortal man come close to embodying his rival god, and the entire Mexican civilization still reeled from the disastrous after effects of that ill fated meeting. *Huitzilopochtli* would never allow that to happen again, and tonight, once he personally sent *Quetzalcoatl* safely to hell, the gods would be more than pleased and bless them with another age of peace.

Huitzilopochtli left *Quetzalcoatl's* quarters, and walked back to his temple, where he began his cleansing rituals in preparation for tonight.

Eagle Warriors stood outside the temple, flanked by the secondary fleet of Jaguar Warriors. More and more of the organization arrived hourly to ready themselves for the final battle.

Huitzilopochtli walked toward the door to his inner chamber.

An Eagle Warrior stopped him, bowed. "Great One, I must show you something." He handed the leader a folded newspaper.

The leader opened it and saw the article on the front page: *Young Stabbing Victim Barely Survives. No Suspects.* He studied the smiling picture of the lanky teenager who appeared too familiar for comfort. The heat of his rage burned from the deepest parts of him. He gritted his teeth and smiled. "Thank you Warrior. Now get back to work."

"Yes, *Senor*." He saluted.

Huitzilopochtli crumpled the paper in his hand and burned it in the nearby fire before retiring to his chamber where he would unfortunately need to make a phone call before preparing himself for the evening.

***

The man in the black El Dorado parked one block off the *Zocalo* facing the Palacio. He woke up earlier than normal today and had his eyes closed when his cell phone rang. "*Hola?*"

"Did you take care of what I asked you to last night, or not?"

"*Si*, I told you."

"Are you *sure*?"

"*Si.*"

"Did you happen to read the paper this morning?"

"Uh, no."

"And where are you now?"

The man gulped. A strangely unsettling feeling hit him in his gut. Something went wrong. He knew it. "Uh…"

The man laughed. "Is that you sitting on the corner of the *Zocalo* in your car?"

"*Si.*"

"Good. Do me a favor, will you?"

"*Si.*"

"Roll down your window."

The streets started to get crowded this morning. He rolled his window down. "Okay."

"It's done?"

"*Si.*"

"Good. Now hold your cell in your left hand and rest it on the car door."

"Okay, hang on, boss." He held the phone in his hand, palm up. *This seemed really stupid…*

"*Hola.*" A fat man in sunglasses stepped off the sidewalk and came around to the driver's side window and lifted his cloth covered hand to reveal the barrel of a gun.

By the time the driver registered what was happening, the bullet pierced his forehead. His fingers opened and he dropped the phone outside his car on to the street.

The fat man picked it up with a gloved hand, slipped it in his jacket and walked into the crowded city center. He held the cell up to his ear. "*Hola.*"

"I heard it. Thank you."

"*No problemo.*"

"Now get going before anyone sees you and bring that phone to me."

Forty Four

M ario finally sat on a bench in the center of the Plaza de la Constitucion and studied his map. He wanted to go to the north to explore the temples there, but realized full well with the clock ticking, his next move better yield more tangible results. His other problem involved transportation. Mario lived in Mexico City all his life, and like many, he used public transport. Today he realized that might be a problem time-wise, but even if he could find a car, which seemed highly unlikely, he hadn't driven anywhere in so long, he wasn't exactly sure how to get there.

His stomach growled. He smelled the food cooking in the street vendor's carts. From one end of the square to the other, he watched excited summer *touristas* shopping in the city center. His mouth started to water and he realized he needed to eat before doing anything else.

Mario considered his dining options and continued to wonder how in the world he could ever possibly find the Presidente in time. With bad roads and no car, he needed a nothing short of a miracle. He never needed a car before. Public transportation served most of the people in the city. He briefly reconsidered taking the subway, but that might take too long. What if his hunch was wrong? He didn't have time for error, and today in particular, he couldn't walk long distances from a metro or bus station and make a dozen stops along the way. This was a matter of life and death. Mario reached under his shirt, pressed his fingertips to his crucifix. "God please help me find a way. Please show me a sign."

Out in the crowded center of the *Zocalo* the daily spectacles of city life are varied. One of the more interesting sites to behold there are the local shaman who purge the citizenry of demons and spirit attachments. Mario saw these would be charlatans out on the square ever since he could remember and rarely gave them a second thought.

Using only a chant and a smoking sage wand bound by string, these self ordained priests work tirelessly to cast demons from the people of Mexico City. Many of the more superstitious residents believed in their work, while others like Mario, believed they took advantage of the weak and poor by praying on their fears.

One of the better known practitioners is a man known only by his first name, Ramon, who claimed to be a sixth generation shaman and direct descendant of *Quetzalcoatl* himself.

Mario normally chuckled to himself as he watched Ramon, but today, after the bizarre death of his sister, his amusement turned to suspicion. Anyone who publicly advertised himself as an *Aztec Healer* needed further investigation.

Although his family was highly spiritual and believed in miraculous happenings and faith healings, no member of the Martinez family ever enlisted the services of such a healer, preferring instead to turn their troubles over to Christ and the Catholic Church.

Today would be the exception to the rule. While Mario watched with intense curiosity, people lined up one by one for Ramon's blessings. He decided to go ahead and pay for one of these ritualistic cleansings, so he could get closer to Ramon. Maybe, just maybe, Ramon knew about the temples and who was responsible for the murder and kidnapping.

He waited for the right moment and watched two other healers work their magic and salesmanship on the Palacio side of the *Zocalo*. He studied their every move, the way they spoke to the people, the methods they used, the costumes they wore. Once he saw a slight break in the line, Mario made his move.

Ramon's Aztec sign stood on an easel directly behind him. He waved to a mother and daughter, trying to persuade them to try a healing. He wore a thick peacock headdress and a leather skirt, moccasins, turquoise beads, and little else. Dark tattoos of ancient symbols covered the top half of his chest and back. His teeth were black and rotting, his eyes were multicolored flecks of brown and gold, his long thin nose had a ring through one side.

Ramon and the other healers never required anyone to pay a single *peso* for any of their services. There were no set prices either, although the implication suggested those who contributed to the till would somehow please the gods, and have a better chance of being cleansed of any unwanted energies.

Mario reached in his pocket and dropped his spare change into Ramon's basket. The sound of the money apparently attracted his attention.

Ramon turned around immediately, waved to Mario, and gestured him toward the front of the growing crowd. He began to chant in the old language, and waved the smudging stick over Mario's body. He drew his hands near Mario's heart and a haunted expression crossed his face. He dramatically swayed back and forth, as if falling. Backing off, he frantically waved his arms around and a strong cloud of smoke filled the air. "There is a death." Ramon lifted his hands to the heavens. "Death is around you. Horrible, horrible death. All around."

He assumed this whole show was a hoax, but had to admit Ramon's insights startled him, scared him even. He wanted to back away and run, tell Ramon he was wrong, but he couldn't. Something told him to stay, despite the fact he didn't want to draw any more unnecessary attention to himself in such a public space.

Did Ramon actually see the terrible recent events of Mario's life, or did he merely want to pretend he did, to attract more customers? He couldn't tell.

The healer flailed about, chanting and issuing verbal warnings to the unseen forces ruining Mario's life.

He hoped Ramon would stop his nonsense right now, stop trying to bring the darkness and pain currently lurking in his heart to light in front of so many people, but regardless of how much he wanted to run away, he stayed. He kept still, waiting to see what else Ramon would do, and if any useful information would come from the strange ceremony.

Ramon closed his eyes once more, chanted and danced around Mario, while a half a dozen onlookers watched him pass the second round of smoke over his back and shoulders."Your sister. I see your sister. She is dead." Ramon opened his eyes and stared him right in the face. His eyes grew wide, like he'd seen a ghost. Another big gust of smoke filled the air as more supposed negativity was brought to the surface and removed. "The *Aztecas* cursed your family. Your family is cursed!" His eyes glazed over and he kept repeating the phrase, either for dramatic effect or to reinforce the idea to Mario himself.

Mario wished he would stop saying these things so loud around so many other people. He didn't want anyone to know what happened. The more Ramon kept talking, the angrier Mario became until finally, he grabbed the little man by the arms, threw him to the ground. "What the hell do you know about my family you son-of-a-bitch?"

Ramon lifted his hands to the air like a man under arrest while several shocked onlookers observed.

Mario wasn't swayed by his feigned fear. He grabbed his shoulders and pulled his face within a few inches of his. "I swear you better tell me what you know right now."

The little man stared back at Mario through bloodshot eyes and began to plead for his life. "I don't know anything, *amigo*, I promise. I am only telling you what is coming to me at this time. I swear it. I saw it in the smoke, *amigo*. It's all there."

Now a crowd gathered around, so Mario pulled Ramon to his feet. "Tell me your name."

"Ramon." The little man pointed to his sign which read *Ancient Aztec healings by Ramon.* He smiled a semi-toothless grin.

"That's your *real name*?"

"*Si.*"

"Come on Ramon, get your sign and your things. You're coming with me." Mario pulled him by his beads and dragged him away.

"But I can't. I have customers," he complained.

Mario grabbed his sign and flipped it over on the concrete. "There. You're officially on break. Come on."

Forty Five

Bene vaguely remembered the warm sponge bath he had before drifting off to sleep. Now he felt someone twisting and turning him. He groggily opened his eyes.

The girl sat next to him on a stool and busily rubbed his bare arms with some kind of oil or lotion. He glanced at the beams in the ceiling, noticed they hadn't changed, but something else had. He felt cold, freezing in fact, and his teeth knocked together so hard they gave him a splitting headache.

"*Hola*," the girl smiled. "You need more of this. It will help. I will cover you soon when I am finished."

"No," Bene finally managed. "Pleeeaaasseee…"

She laughed. "Don't worry. You shake because you're hungry and chilled. You would not eat, remember? If you don't eat, you will get more of this." She held up the familiar container and spoon.

Even the slightest movement caused Bene to feel like his skull would crack in two. He needed something to ease his pain. "Fffoood."

"Oh, so you want to eat now? Good." She reached over him with a piece of bread. "Here you go."

To Bene, the girl's face changed drastically since last time he saw her. She appeared in his mind's eye like someone in a carnival mirror, her once normal features now appeared twisted and deformed, her smiled enlarged and showcased jagged teeth. When she came close to him, the teeth seemed ominous and he wondered if she might bite him. This can't be real, he tried to tell himself, but the closer she came, the more horrible she appeared, "Agh." He cried, but despite his fear, he let her put the bread in his mouth anyway. It tasted like chalk, so thick and dry, he started to choke.

The girl lifted his head. He watched her, but now, instead of her normal pleasant face, her eyes bulged from her tiny head, as if they might pop into the floor at any moment. "Good, you are eating. Take a sip of this."

"No."

"It's only water, *Senor*. Drink, *por favor*." She lifted a cup to his mouth and half of the contents splashed his shivering body. "Oh no. Now I have to redo this." She dabbed his torso with a bright blue cloth.

Bene recalled this bright blue color exactly like the man's face the other day. "Pleeeaassee," he croaked again.

The girl took this to mean he wanted more food. She tore off a smaller piece of the bread and popped it into his mouth.

He tried to eat, but his tongue felt heavy and thick. He sucked on it to avoid the terrible feeling of choking, but it tasted so horrible, it proved almost unbearable. Finally, it softened in his mouth and he swallowed. "Heelllpp meeee."

"You will be okay. I am helping you, see?" She held up a cloth dabbed in the bright blue paint. "I am preparing you for ceremony, doing what I am told." She leaned closer, smiled and laughed. "You're fine, see?"

To Bene, her high pitched laughter sounded like that of a mental patient, her once small teeth took on even more of a jagged appearance than they had moments ago, like some wild animal in the jungle or recently let out of its cage. He continued to try and tell himself this wasn't real. She was an innocent young girl, forced into evil against her will. The fact she now seemed evil, well, that could not be her fault. If needed, Bene must close his eyes and try to talk some sense into her.

There were so many complex things Bene wanted to discuss with her right now, but his mind still felt far too slow to form words of any consequence. Obviously someone brainwashed the girl into thinking her actions justified. She needed to be rescued the same as anyone else around here, even if she'd been morphed into a monster. "Ahhhh…" he mumbled and realized his ability to talk

would soon fade back into nothing. The food. She hid
something in the food. He knew it, but he had no idea
what. His head started spinning again and soon he would
lose consciousness. He hoped she wouldn't try and gnaw
him to death with her prickly teeth while he slept.

"*Quetzalcoatl*," she said matter-of-factly. "You will
soon be out of your misery and one with eternal life."

Forty Six

Mario and Ramon crossed the *Zocalo* and went
into McDonalds where he escorted the Aztec
healer up to the counter, pointed to the menu.
"What do you want?"

Ramon seemed shocked. "What?"

"I'll buy your food, so tell me what you want."

Ramon's eyes lit up. "Really?" He ordered the biggest
meal on the menu.

They each took their Big Mac meals and found a seat in
the back corner of the crowded restaurant. "I am working
with El Presidente Juarez and we need your help."

"Oh *Quetzalcoatl*." Ramon smiled.

Mario scratched his head. "*Que?*"

Ramon bit in to his burger. "*Quetzalcoatl*, you know,
Benito Juarez?"

"No, I don't."

"*Si*, that's what we call him."

"Who's *we*?"

"My people, the Aztecs."

Mario felt even more confused. "Why?"

Ramon bit in to his burger, special sauce dripped down his chin. "Because he looks like him."

"Wait just a minute. How could Benito Juarez look like an Aztec god?"

Ramon laughed. "You not read, brother? This is our heritage."

Mario felt foolish for not concentrating on his studies in school. "Tell me."

"*Quetzalcoatl* is the feathered serpent. He is a man god with clear white skin, a beard...Ever since Benito got elected, some of our people said he might be—"

Mario nearly spit his burger out. "You mean you actually believe he is *Quetzalcoatl* returned?"

Ramon shrugged. "I don't know if I do..."

"But you're saying *your people* do?"

"*Si,* prophecy says *Quetzalcoatl* will return to usher in a new age of peace. You remember reading about Cortez?"

He really didn't. "Tell me."

"The Aztecs thought Cortez was *Quetzalcoatl*. Turned out he killed them all, even Montezuma, and destroyed the entire Aztec civilization. Some of my people believe the real *Quetzalcoatl* will soon return. It's written in the stars."

Mario grabbed a wad of fries, stuffed them in his mouth. He had an eerie feeling this sick belief system might be linked to Benito's disappearance.

"So, how can I possibly help *El Presidente Quetzalcoatl*?" Ramon spoke with a full mouth, hungrily devouring his food.

Mario didn't want to divulge anything private to this stranger, but he knew he needed to at least pretend to confide completely in him, if he was going to get answers,

"What I'm about to tell you is top secret. You can't tell anyone, *comprende*?"

Ramon nodded, his mouth full of fries. "Mmm hmm."

He leaned over the table, whispered. "My sister was murdered two days ago, just like you said."

"Ah ha, I knew it!" He pointed a french-fry in the air.

Mario didn't have time to praise Ramon for his intuitive abilities. "I found her in Templo Mayor. Did you hear about it?"

Ramon shook his head. "I live on the streets, in my car. I hear a lot, but nothing about any murder."

"She was brutally executed, beheaded, and her body parts were removed in a ceremony similar to those performed by the ancient Aztecs."

Ramon listened intently to the details of the death and nodded his head in recognition. "I know of such rituals. Nobody used these since the times of our ancestors."

Mario scowled. "Are you involved with this?"

"No," Ramon's eyes widened.

"You sure?"

"I swear on my mother's life."

Mario sized him up and believed he was telling the truth. "Do you know anyone who performs sacrifices?"

Ramon nervously stuffed his mouth full of hamburger and stared at the crossword puzzle on his placemat.

"Listen here, Ramon," Mario smacked his hand on the table. "This is serious. I need you to help *El Presidente* and I put a stop to this before more innocent people die, *comprende*? If you know anything about anyone …"

Ramon sat silently and stared down at what was left of his fries. "I don't know, *amigo*." He sipped his Coke. "It's dangerous."

"Of course it is," Mario said. "That's why we're willing to pay you more money than you have probably ever seen in your life to help us." He discreetly reached in his pocket and flashed a wad of cash under the table.

Ramon's face lit up. "*Si...*"

"Do you think you could earn this?" Mario held the money out just beyond his reach.

Ramon's enthusiasm for the project seemed to grow. "Si."

He snapped the money back and put it away. "This is the deal. Do you know anything about anyone who might want to perform this kind of ritual? If you do, who?"

Ramon polished off the last bite of burger. "There is a group of powerful men I've only heard about. I've never seen them. Nobody has. They call themselves *El Templo*. They are a secret society interested in preserving the old ways and honoring the old gods."

Mario could hardly believe his ears. "How do I find them? Where do they operate? Can you take me there now?"

Ramon laughed. "Oh *amigo*...they operate everywhere and anywhere."

"How do I find them? I want to talk to them, see what makes them tick, find out where they meet..."

"*Amigo, El Templo* hide in plain sight. It's tough to reach these men. Some even wonder if they are real or merely a myth, an urban legend."

"What do you think?"

Ramon shrugged. "I don't know. Probably real."

"You're not a member?"

"Oh no, *Senor*." Ramon sipped his Coke. "Not me. This is secret."

"Where do they meet?"

Ramon shrugged. "*Yo no se*. I told you. Nobody knows. Like I said, it's secret."

"Do you think this *El Templo* group, based on what you've heard about them, would hold a grudge against a *Presidente* if they believed he actually was their returned god Quetzalcoatl? I mean would they have it in for him?"

"*Si*. Of course. They are *Huitzilopochtli* worshippers, from what I hear. He is god of war and sacrifice. *Quetzalcoatl* is god of peace, but you probably know that already."

He didn't. "Listen," he whispered. "I heard they had a big meeting yesterday out at one of the big Aztec temples. I need to get out there today. Do you have any idea which temple they might use?" Mario had his own hunch, but he wanted Ramon's opinion.

Ramon wadded up his napkins, twisted them around in his hands. "There's only two I can think of."

"Which ones?"

"Teotihuacan, the Temples of the Sun and the Moon. That would be a good place for a large crowd, or Cholula. That is a good one too, or…"

Mario rolled his eyes. "I'm running out of time, Ramon. Which of the two do you think is more likely?"

"Teotihuacan, for sure. It's closer to town, and like I said, the *El Templo* organization is pretty well connected in the city, from what I've heard." Ramon held out his hand for the cash. "Plus there's a temple to the feathered serpent there."

"Feathered serpent?"

"You know, *Quetzalcoatl*." Ramon leaned closer to Mario, stretching his skinny hand to the paper where Mario's fries were sitting.

"Here. Have them." Mario pushed his fries over to Ramon, who gobbled them up.

"*Gracias*."

Mario stood up and dumped his trash. "Do you know how to get to Teotihuacan?"

Ramon shook his head. "No *amigo*, I told you. I live in my car."

"Your *car*?"

"Si."

Mario smiled for the first time all day.

Forty Seven

With his face painted red as the blood and hearts he demanded, *Huitzilopochtli* stood atop the pyramid on the platform and raised the heart of the Eagle Warrior, his latest victim, up to the gods. "*Vive Huitzilopochtli*."

By now, hundreds of robed and feathered people gathered. Some danced in circles playing drums and other instruments, while others chanted in the ancient tongue and cheered with delight at the coming enlightenment.

"Tonight we will move to the sacred site, we will march openly in the streets, and we will offer the ultimate sacrifice to our hungry god."

The drumming grew ever louder, clouds of incense smoke filled the air and the crowd jumped with joy.

"Ladies and gentlemen, allow me to unveil your god, *Quetzalcoatl*."

Two of the largest Eagle Warriors stepped out with a wooden cart they wheeled to the base of the pyramid. The contents were covered in blankets until they carried it up the steps and set it on the stone altar.

The leader ceremoniously removed the cloth, revealing a near lifeless Benito. "I present *Quetzalcoatl*."

***

Bene heard screaming and clapping, but his body felt totally numb, even worse than before. The hot sun prickled his skin, mercilessly burning his half naked body.

"*Attencion*! Today is an important day for our future. We will worship our god freely for the next two hours and then we will make our way to the sacred site where we will make our offering to please our gods. I look forward to each one of you coming out this evening, participating and joining our celebration as we prepare for the next period of peace. *Vive Quetzalcoatl*."

"*Vive Quetzalcoatl*."

The leader lifted a wooden staff with an obsidian blade attached to one end and chanted. "*Vive Huitzilopochtli*."

The crowd jumped in the air and echoed his call. "*Vive Huitzilopochtli*."

"*Excellente*. Enjoy this day. I will see you tonight."

Forty Eight

Mario left Ramon out in front of McDonalds with cash in hand and a hot apple pie. He took the car keys, donned his sunglasses, and ran across the *Zocalo* to a parking garage under one of the hotels, where he found Ramon's beat up old Pinto covered in parking tickets. He peeled them off the windows and drove to the parking garage attendant, holding out a few pesos.

"Ah *Senor*," the attendant said. "This car is long overdue on parking."

"Will this cover it?" He held out a large wad of cash. She smiled. "*Si*."

"Open the gate now and you can keep the change."

"Oh *gracias*."

Mario sped away.

***

On the way to Teotihuacan, Mario realized he'd never driven here before. Several years ago he visited the temples with his parents and sister, but they rode a bus.

One of the most famous archeological wonders in the world, Teotihuacan was home to the Pyramid of the Sun, the third largest in the world, and the slightly smaller Pyramid of the Moon. The two monuments were connected by the *Calle de los Muertos* or *street of the dead*. The Aztec holy site seemed a logical place for performing ritual sacrifice.

Despite the fact this site had hundreds of daily visitors, Mario realized the El Templo organization could easily slip into any of the dozens of subterranean caverns, where it would be possible for all kinds of heinous acts to go completely unnoticed, if they were performed underground or inside a temple complex. His problem was he had no idea how to get into the Temple of the Feathered Serpent, assuming it was open to the general public.

He drove on to the grounds and passed a bus stop before driving the remaining half mile or so to the large paved visitor's parking lot near the entrance to the site. Even this spot was quite a distance from the front gate, and he felt thankful to have access to a car today. He turned off the ignition, locked the door and ran in the sweltering heat to the main entrance. He paid for his admission ticket, and noticed a friendly young girl in the booth. He figured he better start asking anyone and everyone he could. "Which way to the temple of the Feathered Serpent?"

"Right behind us." She turned and pointed to the closest stone structure in the entire complex. "Here's a map."

"Great, thanks." Mario grabbed the map and stuffed it in his pocket and started jogging down the rocky path. He didn't realize how far away everything was out here. Miles separated the monument, even though they looked close together thanks to their colossal size. Once he felt completely out of breath, he reached the front of pyramid dedicated to Quetzalcoatl which seemed a fraction of the size of the more spectacular Sun and Moon monuments. He climbed the front façade all the way to the top, searching the ground for any blood or other evidence, but didn't see a thing. On the back side, the familiar sight of scaffolding held together a crumbling chamber down below which he couldn't see into from his present vantage point.

He carefully climbed down the steps, getting a little dizzy from the heights, and ran around to the back to get a closer look. Nothing.

He ran out to the *Calle de los Muertos* and glanced down the mile plus long road toward the Pyramids of the Sun and Moon. Two loaded tour busses since arrived, carrying at least a hundred visitors. This couldn't be the place. These murderers were bold, true, but they couldn't possibly carry out their plans with so many people around. He came all the way out here though, so he would run and check quickly. It was possible Benito was here at some point, even if they moved him to a new location.

"I have to find you Bene, and I will do it, no matter what." Mario called into the wind and sprinted down the long gravel road toward the pyramids to see what else he would discover.

Forty Nine

Igh atop the platform amidst a cloud of incense, the Great One dismissed his congregation after several hours of ceremony. "It is time to move toward our final spot. Drive carefully and we will meet again in a few hours."

Once the crowd cleared, *Huitzilopochtli* enlisted the assistance of two of his largest Eagle Warriors, who accompanied him to the room where the god rested after his afternoon debut.

The little girl sat in the corner on a wooden stool watching *Quetzalcoatl* sleep.

Huitzilopochtli called to her. "Daughter."

The little girl jumped to her feet when she saw him and stood at attention. "Yes, father?"

"Have you given our god the *pulque* he requires for this journey?"

"No father. He did not want it."

"What? How dare you disobey?" He stepped closer and raised a hand to strike.

The girl cowered in the corner and shielded herself with her hands. "I promise, papa, I will do it now. Give me a few more minutes."

He slapped the girl so hard across the face, she fell to the ground. "Enough! You have one minute to get it down his miserable throat, or else you'll be joining him tonight. *Comprende*?"

She cried and crawled to his feet. "Please, Father. Come back in a moment. Let me gather the *pulque* and take care of him."

"We don't have much time, so hurry." He stormed out, slamming the door behind him.

***

The slamming door woke Benito from a deep sleep. He cracked his eyes open and realized he felt more mentally capable now and during the past few hours than he had since coming here. His head still pounded, but overall, the drug hidden in his bread proved nowhere near as potent as the dreaded *pulque*.

He heard the girl sobbing and shuffling something around on the floor. He saw her standing near a table, preparing his evening drink. "Hey," he whispered.

At first she didn't hear him above the roar of the cars in the parking area outside.

"Hey," he repeated.

She stopped and turned to him. "You're awake." She wiped the tears from her face.

Benito noticed a black bruise on her cheek that wasn't there before. "Are you okay?"

Her eyes fell to the floor. "*Si.*"

He wished he could help the poor thing. To think these monsters would harm a child was unthinkable, but after all they'd done so far, Bene realized he could expect nothing less. "You're sure?"

She ignored the question and mixed the *pulque*. A few globs dribbled down the side of a thick wooden cup. She wiped off with the edge with her blouse and walked slowly toward him, careful not to spill another drop.

Benito needed to talk some sense into her if he expected to survive this ordeal. "Please don't make me drink that."

The girl sat on the edge of the bed and moved the cup toward his lips. "I have no choice. I must give you this or I will be among the first to die tonight."

"*Por favor*, please don't…"

"I think it is best. You won't feel the pain once they…" She glanced down at his sheets, unable to keep eye contact.

She has a conscience. Benito might convince her to help him if he handled this right. If not, he would be in a far more debilitating stupor than any he'd experienced thus far and could count out any chance of surviving this mess. "How about we pretend I took it? I can act sleepy. I promise I won't tell."

She shook her head. "My father would find out. He's a very smart man."

Father? Horrified to think any parent would subject their child to such treachery, Benito had to know more. "Who? Who's your father?"

The girl pulled back the curtain, pointed outside to the feathered man who barked orders to guards. "Him."

Bene's blood ran cold. He realized he would not be able to say anything against the tyrant for fear it would further alienate the girl. "I see…well, I still believe I could pretend. Don't you ever play with toys and pretend things?"

"I'm too old for that. Papa said so." She held a hand on his forehead and started to tip the cup into his mouth. "Now drink this or I'll go get my daddy."

Benito drew a deep breath and with all the force of strength left within him, he lifted his limp arm and swung it at the cup, knocking it into the floor and hitting her in the side of the face in the process.

She jumped and let out a small scream. "Hey. Don't do that." She brushed her bruised cheek with her hand. "Ouch.".

"I'm sorry, I didn't mean to do that. I only wanted to stop you from giving me that drink. Did your papa do that to you?"

Her eyes fell to the floor, she shook her head and went back to the table, poured some more *pulque* and set it aside and grabbed a wooden board from the dirt floor. She carried it over to the bedside and lifted it above her head, about to swing. "Sorry, but this is for your own good."

Bene leaned his head back in the pillows, hoping she wouldn't knock him out. "Please, no. You don't have to—"

Like a star batter in a girl's softball league, the little girl swung, fortunately not at his head, but his hand.

Benito cried out in agony as he heard the sound of his left hand and wrist shattering. His head fell back on his pillow.

She threw the board aside, picked up the pulque and slowly walked toward him, holding the spoon up. "Now open up, and let's get this over with, okay?"

***

Juarez Senior paced frantically around Rita's office. "Where in the world is Martinez? What do you think he's doing?"

"I don't know, *Senor* Juarez."

"Well, call him and find out."

"I tried several times, *Senor* Juarez, but he doesn't answer."

"Then try him again. I need my son back."

"I'm sure he realizes that, *Senor*." Rita reminded him.

"Then call him," Juarez demanded.

She picked up her phone. "Si, *Senor*."

***

The busy executive picked up his phone and dialed. A man answered. "Hello?"

"What is going on with Mario Martinez?"

"He isn't a problem."

"How do you know?"

"He is a non-issue."

"Are you sure? I need answers."

"Right now he's wandering around *Teotihuacan*. He's way off the trail now. All systems are go. Nothing will stop us."

"You'd better be right." He hung up and stared down into *La Plaza de la Constitucion*.

Fifty

Mario ran to both the pyramids of the Sun and Moon, checked all around and underneath them and found absolutely no evidence of anything out of the ordinary. A sinking feeling settled in his heart when he thought about how much time he wasted here. If he didn't hurry, there would be no hope for Bene.

He hurried back toward the front gates and noticed the same girl at the ticket counter. Maybe she could help. Dripping in sweat by the time he reached her, he sucked in air, calmed his breathing. "Have you seen any people out here the past few days wearing any kind of strange costumes?"

She frowned. "No, *Senor*."

"Are you sure?"

She gave him a strange look. "*Si*."

"Darn." Mario slapped his hands on his thighs. "I didn't think so."

"Why? What are you looking for?"

"I heard about a festival going on this week, an Aztec ritual reenactment, I really wanted to see in person."

The girl shrugged. "I don't know anything about that. Sorry."

Mario sighed. "Okay, *gracias*." He started to walk away when he noticed a gift shop to his right. He stepped inside, noticed an older lady busy in the back, and another younger girl selling candy in the front. He walked up, put a pack of gum on the counter and paid. "Excuse me. Do you know about any festivals going on this week out here?"

The young girl pointed to a door behind her. "No. If you want that kind of information, you need to ask the *Senora* in the back. She's my boss."

The older lady seemed distracted, ill tempered, or both, but he had no choice. He walked up to her and waited, hoping to catch her attention, but she never turned around. "*Hola*."

She appeared taken aback by his disruption, and stopped working. "*Si?*"

"I need some information about *Quetzalcoatl*."

"It's in your brochure." She turned around and kept counting.

"Ahem…I hate to bother you, *Senor*a, but I heard about an Aztec festival going on out here this week, and—"

She kept her eyes on her project. "No, that's not here."

"Do you know where it is?"

"Si, there is a big group gathered at *Santa Cecilia Acatitlan*." She checked her watch. "They might still be there, if you hurry."

"Is it a festival for *Quetzalcoatl*?"

She kept working. "I don't know, but it is the only festival going on this week in the area."

"Is it a very busy place?" Mario hoped it wasn't as crowded as Teotihuacan or there would be no point checking there.

"No. It's remote. Not too many *touristas* there, but an important archeological site. Now if you'll excuse me…" She disappeared in a room in the back of the shop.

Mario felt renewed hope. He went to the front and the young girl gave him directions. He ran back to the car hoping he would make it to the temple in time and praying to find Bene.

***

Mario finally reached the pyramid of *Santa Cecilia Actitlan* around five in the afternoon and pulled into the gravel lot near the temple. Crunched cans, paper napkins and plastic bottles littered the otherwise pristine environment. Empty containers and trash cluttered the landscape making it look like a county fair or rock concert just let out. There certainly were no signs of a bloody rampage anywhere in the area so either he arrived too late, or the woman at *Teotihuacan* was wrong.

He felt an overwhelming sinking feeling in his gut. He came all the way out here for nothing. Mario looked around. He came all this way and again, he needed to check. Someone here might know what went on here and where everyone went.

He parked Ramon's car and ran up toward the temple. There wasn't much outside except for the litter, but inside the temple, Mario found what looked like fresh blood covering the gravel floor. *Surely not.* Maybe it was phony, all for show, but what if it was real? Mario had no equipment or way to test that now, but at least it appeared like something went on here.

What if they killed Bene? Cold chills ran up his spine at the thought. No. His instincts said Benito was still alive. The kidnappers wanted him for something important.

He spun around, staring at all the interior temple walls for more clues, but his mind felt overwhelmed and distracted by the pending deadline. He stepped outside, took a breath of air and tried to see if anyone was still around.

A row of modest homes stood near the site near a rundown tourist information center.

He ran up the steps, peeked inside the window. Luckily they hadn't closed down for the day yet. Inside, an employee swept the floor while another wiped the windows.

He tried the door. Locked. He pounded his fist on the window and gave a pleading look to the girl with the window cleaner until she reluctantly let him inside.

"*Hola.* Do you know about a festival going on here today or yesterday?" he asked both of the people who worked there.

The girl who let him in didn't say a word.

The boy nodded. "*Si.*"

"Oh good. Will they be back tomorrow?"

"No."

The kid wasn't a lot of help, so Mario decided he would give an incentive. He pulled a few pesos from his pocket, handed them over. "Could you give me some information about it?"

The kid never smiled, but snapped the money from his hands. "*Si.* What do you want to know?"

"For starters, was it an Aztec festival?"

"*Si*."

"What are they celebrating?"

The kid gestured toward a mural on the wall describing an event from the 1500's. "*Aqui, Noche Triste*."

Mario read all about the events of July 1, 1520, when the Aztecs made their final stand against Cortez and the Spaniards. During that event, thousands of Aztecs perished, and it came to be known as the *Night of Sorrows*. He glanced at his watch and noticed the date on the inscription: July 1. His heart nearly stopped. He handed over a few more pesos. "Hey. Do you happen to know where they went this evening?"

He nodded. "*Si. Ciudad de Mexico*."

Mario's heart skipped a beat. "Are you sure?"

"*Si*."

He wondered why they would go there when they could take care of all of their killing out here in the middle of nowhere. This made no sense. "Is there an event tonight?"

"*Yo no se*. It's just what I heard."

"From who?"

The kid pulled a candy bar from the display, opened it and began eating. "From the men who were here. I heard them talking about it."

Why would this event be so important? Again, Mario wished he paid better attention in school. "What did *Noche Triste* mean to the Aztecs?"

The kid led him back to the sign, pointed at the artist's renderings of Cortez. "The *Aztecas* made a final stand against Cortez. They wanted to save their homeland from his rule, but failed. Cortez slaughtered everyone."

The light went on for Mario. "And so they blame Cortez for the downfall of the—"

"*Si*. Cortez destroyed the empire. *Noche Triste* represents the Aztecs, still proud of their heritage, seeking revenge upon Cortez, cursing him forever." The kid turned and walked away.

Oh no! Mario dialed Juarez.

"Where have you been, Martinez? We've been trying to call you all day long." Juarez yelled before Mario could even say hello.

"*Senor* Juarez, I know why they took Benito. Tell me, are there any festivals going on tonight in the *Zocalo*?"

"Si," Juarez said. "Tonight is *Festival de la Virgin de los Remedios*."

Could it be the same? "Any others you know about?"

"No. This is tradition. Every year on July first."

" Is it in the *Zocalo*?"

"*Si* followed by Mass in Cathedral Metropolitano. Rita Benito and I go every year."

Mario panicked. Cathedral Metropolitano sat atop the Aztecs main temple and represented Cortez' defeat of the great civilization. This couldn't be a coincidence. Mario was familiar with similar ceremonies. Normally the people disguised themselves in elaborate costumes and staged elaborate reenactments. *What if...* "No!"

"Why not?"

"You can't go there, *Senor*. I don't have time to explain. When does it start?"

"Mass begins in the next hour or two, I think, right after the parade."

"Parade?"

"*Si*. They are gathering in the streets now."

"Are they in costume?"

"*Si*, all sorts of festival masks, feathers, signs of Virgin Mary. Everyone is on their knees on the way to the Cathedral."

"*Senor* Juarez, it is critical you and Rita do not go to the festival tonight. I fear for your lives. Please listen. "

Juarez sounded incensed. "We always go."

Mario prayed the stubborn Juarez would listen. "Do not go near there tonight. Stay put until you hear from me." Mario hung up the phone and ran.

Fifty One

Father Salazar stood at the altar of the church and laid out fresh candles, Holy water, chalices, incense and communion plates for the evening ceremony. He noticed Sister Hernandez already placed fresh linen out, which he greatly appreciated.

He placed the solid gold ciborium filled with the Eucharist offerings of sacred bread for Holy Communion in the center of the table.

Outside, he heard the impassioned fervor of the people of Mexico City as the pilgrims walked on their knees to the steps of the Cathedral Metropolitano for the special services tonight in honor of *Virgin de los Remedios*.

Her statue sat squarely on the altar. The Virgin effigy held deep spiritual and historic importance for the people of Mexico. Presented as a gift from the Conquistadores, the figure represented the influx of the Spanish with the

Mexican heritage, a celebration of the union of the two people into one. Tonight it was on loan from the chapel bearing her name and would be returned once the ceremonies were over.

Outside the chanting grew ever louder as the choir waited patiently in the wings and the nuns and priests from the parish filed out one by one, singing the Lord's Prayer.

Father Salazar prayed quietly, anticipating the upcoming events of the evening.

"Father Salazar?"

He looked up and saw Sister Hernandez. "*Si*, Sister?"

"Are you ready for this evening?"

"Absolutely. Is the choir prepared with the songs?"

"*Si*, Father. This will be an evening to remember."

Salazar smiled. "I agree."

***

Outside in the streets of Mexico City, a congregation of several hundred donned foot long plumed peacock feather headdresses, masks similar to those worn centuries before by their Aztec ancestors, beaded jewelry and intricately designed face paint. Many arrived by subway, others by bus, some crammed five, six and seven people into their cars, and parked wherever they could find space. Tonight's historic event would unfold for the entire world to see. Each participant believed they were an important part of a shared destiny.

A black sedan with tinted windows carried the leader of the organization, adorned in full regalia, he sat right alongside the official guest of honor.

The car parked and was greeted by four Eagle Warriors, each wearing his finest beads, all with fresh tattoos inscribed especially for tonight. They helped the special guest out of the car, placed him in a pine box. Each man grabbed hold of a handle and lifted the guest high above their heads, while the ruler walked two steps behind, flanked by one Eagle and one Jaguar on each side.

The Great One turned to his attendants. "We have our offerings, *si*?"

"*Si*." The Jaguar pointed out two pine boxes. "In front of us."

"Very good."

They marched into the *Zocalo* past the hundreds of faithful Catholics on their knees in reverence to the statue brought here hundreds of years earlier by the enemy Spaniards.

The leader followed his own procession toward Cathedral Metropolitano where he would finally end the celebration of Cortez and the downfall of the mighty Aztec Empire. The scent of incense filled the air and would soon join with blood and sacrifice. His heart swelled with pride and anticipation. "All is well. Our time has come at long last. Destiny awaits."

***

Benito lay quietly in his makeshift crypt and listened, careful not to move a single muscle for fear his captors might catch on to the fact he was lucid. For some reason this afternoon's dose of *pulque* wasn't as strong as previous mixtures. Maybe the girl did it on purpose to help him, maybe not. Regardless, he was thankful to have some sense about him. With each passing minute, he gained more mental clarity to help carry out his plan.

Once the proper moment presented itself, he would strike and avenge the deaths of his loved ones. By the grace of God, he would succeed, and if not, he would die knowing he tried his best to stop these evil men from harming anyone else.

***

On the other side of the city, Mario sat in a terrible traffic jam and hadn't moved a foot in the past ten minutes. He pounded his hands on the steering wheel, checked his watch. "I need a sign, Lord. Please. Help me."

Just then he noticed a metro station sign on his right and chuckled. "Sorry Ramon." Screeching over two lanes of traffic, Mario parked the Aztec healer's car along a busy street and ran.

Fifty Two

Father Salazar held the cathedral door open for dozens of devotees who climbed the church steps on their knees, weeping in ecstasy for their love of God. The pews filled to capacity, while other pilgrims remained on the floor. The angelic sounds of the choir echoed in the sanctuary and the nuns stood along the wall.

Salazar took his post at the altar, his hands in prayer. "Greetings, welcome. Tonight we offer special blessings for the unification of Mexico and Spain by honoring our beloved *Virgin de los Remedios.* Let us pray."

Salazar bowed his head. Sadly, he noticed the empty seats in the front row reserved for Benito and Stefano

Juarez, although he felt blessed for many things, their absence weighed heavily on his heart.

***

The Great One watched the Cathedral doors close. "Now is time, brothers and sisters. We must march quickly now. Our time has come."

***

Bene felt his box being jostled around. To his surprise, the men removed the coffin lid. It was almost time for him to get up and run. He peeked ever-so-slightly through slits in his eyelids. The chanting and singing sounded familiar. He wondered what day it was, and then it hit him. *Dear God, please don't let any of my loved ones be in church tonight.*

***

Mario pushed his way into the metro car and crammed himself against the door for the entire ride to the *Zocalo*. Rush hour was in full swing, but at least he was moving again. If he stayed on the roads it might've taken hours to reach city center. He closed his eyes, listened to the sound of the cars whizzing on the tracks and prayed he would reach the church in time.

Fifty Three

Moments after Father Salazar began the service, the back doors of Cathedral Metropolitano burst open and a band of costumed people rushed inside. "*Vive Huitzilopochtli.*"

A single dart blown from a reed, as in days of old, flew across the gathering, hitting Father Salazar right between the eyes. The Archbishop fell forward, knocked the ciborium off the table into the crowd. Unbelievably, the bread and wine blessed as the body of Christ splattered in the aisles and a human heart fell out and landed on a woman in the front row. Everyone screamed as mass pandemonium ensued. Hundreds of men rushed the altar, dragging Salazar off to locations unknown.

At that moment, the presumably drugged Benito Juarez covered in bright blue paint stood up, leapt from his make shift throne and threw his arms around a Jaguar Warrior, sending them both to the ground. The warrior's fist sent him immediately back into oblivion.

The leader approached the altar while hundreds of screaming faithful ran for their lives toward the door. "Bring me the offerings now."

The Eagle Warriors came forth, bearing the secondary offerings which were quickly removed from the pine boxes. First, the body of an elderly lady was placed on the altar. The ruler lifted his obsidian blade, and pierced the already lifeless chest cavity and held up the heart for all to see. "*Vive Huitzilopo*chtli."

His followers pushed their way toward the front of the sanctuary echoed. "*Vive Huitzilopochtli.*"

Two Eagle Warriors grabbed the old woman's lifeless body, rushed past the panicked crowd, and tossed her down the outer steps of the cathedral. In true Aztec form, the body rolled toward the bottom of the steps, landing in the street below. Shocked onlookers screamed out in horror.

Next, the secondary offering appeared near the altar. Two Jaguar Warriors lifted the headless remains of Angela Martinez from the pine box and tossed her ceremoniously down the cathedral steps, where she came to rest on the upper landing outside.

The leader glanced around, waiting, watching, expecting. "Where is our god? Bring him to me now."

Two Eagle Warriors disappeared into the back to fetch Benito while the Catholic congregation who were still trapped inside the church continued to scream and tried to escape.

***

When the subway finally stopped at the station nearest to Templo Mayor, Mario ran as fast as his legs could carry him, past the street vendors he normally saw in the mornings, around the corner, and into the crowded *Zocalo*. He pushed past dozens of people headed straight for the Cathedral.

Mario immediately saw the commotion near the front steps of the Cathedral. Two dead bodies, torn to shreds, were lying on the steps. People frantically cried out. He ran up the steps, drew his weapon and forced the church doors open.

Inside the cathedral, a crazed maniac stood near the front altar surrounded by hundreds of costumed freaks. "*Vive Huitzilopochtli*." He held an obsidian blade up to the sky.

Mario couldn't believe his eyes. There, flat on his back, palms open to the heavens was the limp body of Benito Juarez.

The man lowered his blade toward Benito's heart. "*Vive Huitzilopochtli.*"

"Stop!" Mario drew his gun and fired.

Fifty Four

S tabbing pain pierced through the leader's turquoise beads, through skin and muscle, straight into his heart, and pushed out his back. The crimson he worshipped in life gushed forth from his own body. He fell backwards down the stairs.

Several shocked costumed guards drew their weapons and turned toward Mario. They held seven foot long wooden spears, all tipped with sharp obsidian blades and charged straight for him.

***

"Stop or you'll all die." Mario held his weapon high, feeling relatively confident since the warriors appeared to be armed with primitive weapons.

The men were not deterred by the gun, instead they continued toward Mario.

Mario turned to the remaining few people in the church. "Get down everyone." He fired a straight line from left to right, and one by one, five of the fiercest men he ever encountered in his life fell to the ground. Dead.

Suddenly a sixth man came out of nowhere and raised a shorter obsidian blade at Benito, who was still tied down on the altar. Without hesitating, Mario shot him between the eyes, rushed to Bene's side. "Thank God you're okay. I thought you were dead."

Bene managed a faint smile. "Me too."

Mario untied Bene and grabbed his left hand to help him up.

"Agh!" Bene cried out in pain.

Mario saw his left hand cracked open, a bone showed through the skin. "Sorry. We're going to get you to a hospital." He put his arm around Bene's shoulder, and braced him while he tried to sit up. "You okay?"

Benito looked like hell, but he was alive, and that was all that mattered. "Uh huh. Call my father, will you?"

Mario handed Bene his phone. "Here you take it. I need to secure things." He glanced around the Cathedral. The terrorists were already long gone. He'd love to send them all to prison, but couldn't identify them because of their elaborate disguises. A few nuns huddled in a corner, crying, but other than that, all appeared clear. He returned to Benito. "Did you get ahold of your father?"

"*Si*. He's on his way." Bene stood up, slowly at first, and threw his arms around Mario. "Thank you, brother. Thank you for not giving up on me."

"I'll always have your back."

"Likewise." Bene's eyes watered with emotion. He scanned the church.

Mario wanted to get Benito out of here to safety as quickly as possible, but he wouldn't budge. "What is it?"

Still in shock, Benito stared at the body of the masked leader. "Before we go, I need to see something." He walked over to his torturer, removed his mask and gasped.

"What?"

Bene fell to his knees. "This is Judge Pena."

The name meant nothing to Mario. "Who?"

"He is – I mean *was* – one of our closest family friends. I can't believe it." Bene crawled to his feet, put his hand to his head. "Oh that hurts."

Mario helped him into a pew. "Listen, you need to go to the hospital right away. I'll call an ambulance."

"My dad will have a fit when he finds out about Pena. What are we going to do, Mario? How are we going to fight these people? This isn't over, you know. Did you see all of them? They came out of nowhere and now they disappeared again."

Mario agreed. Like cockroaches, they crawled from the deepest parts of the city wreaking havoc in all directions.

"Bene? Benito?" Juarez Senior and Rita shouted when they saw them.

"Benito." His father ran t him and held him close. "Thank God you're safe."

Bene grabbed his father's neck. "Papa, I'm sorry about what I said. Please forgive me."

"Always son," he cried. "I am just happy you are safe."

Rita blew her nose in a handkerchief and threw her arms around Mario's neck. "Thank you. I knew you'd find him."

Mario smiled. "I got lucky, *Senora*."

"No, Mario. You have a gift. *Gracias*." Rita wiped her tears.

Fifty Five

A mbulance personnel arrived on the scene and checked Bene out to make sure he was okay. Other than the shattered hand, a gash in the head, dehydration and a few other cuts, scrapes and bruises, Benito would be okay.

"How is he?" Juarez Senior asked a paramedic.

"Fine. We'll take him to the hospital for observation."

"I am coming with you." Juarez turned to Bene. "I won't let you out of my sight from here on out."

They packed Bene securely on the stretcher. "Want to ride with us to the hospital, Mario?"

He did, more than anything, but with all the commotion, only one person came to his mind – Elsa. "I'll stop by later. Right now, I have my own family business to deal with."

Before they left, Juarez Senior came up to Mario, shook his hand. "I can't thank you enough for what you've done."

"No thanks needed. Bene is family. My sister is gone, but I have a brother now."

Juarez patted him on the back. "Thank you."

Policia swarmed the scene and scraped the remains of the two bodies off the Cathedral steps. Mario recognized them both and his eyes welled with tears. Angela and Rosa could finally be laid to rest. Seeing his sister's corpse was awful, but at least he kept his word to bring her home. Elsa would be relieved.

Mario still felt the sting of shock at how many warriors threatened his life tonight. His quick shooting saved Bene's life. Although Angela was long gone from this world, he liked to think she watched over him now, happy he saved the man she loved.

He pulled his cell from his pocket and called his mother. "Mama, I found Bene. He's alive."

"Thank God! Where are you? I'm about ready to leave the hospital now."

"Okay, I'll be right—" A bloodcurdling scream from inside the Cathedral interrupted his thoughts. "Uh…on second thought, give me a few minutes."

"What was that noise?" his mother asked.

The screaming got louder.

"Nothing. Stay put. I'll be there soon." Mario ran up the Cathedral steps toward the shouting.

An altar boy who couldn't be older than eight or nine ran outside screaming, his pure white robe splattered in blood. "Help! Please somebody help!"

Mario grabbed the boy by the shoulders. "Are you okay? What is it?"

Nearly out of breath, the little boy continued. "Father Salazar. They took Father Salazar."

"Who?"

"The men in the masks."

Mario's blood ran cold. Although Benito was safe, there was much more work to do before his sister's killers would be brought to justice. He glanced up at the Cathedral, down at the Zocalo below and turned to follow the boy into the church.

To Be Continued…

About the Author

Annette Shelley is a lifelong sci-fi and horror fan and author of several novels and short stories. She loves living in the worlds she creates.

Visit Annette online:
www.annetteshelley.com

DO YOU LOVE TO TRAVEL?

Visit www.redskytravelandtours.com
Sign up to receive weekly travel specials on this link:

http://www.redskytravelandtours.com/
traveldeals/optin

Be one of the first people notified when Annette Shelley leads one of her amazing trips to destinations around the world!

www.ingramcontent.com/pod-product-compliance
Lightning Source LLC
Chambersburg PA
CBHW072103170626
46813CB00004B/1445